Shot Through the Tart

Laughing Loaf Bakery Mystery #7

Victoria Kazarian

To Pete

Chapter One

A power drill droned, then revved up to a shrill, ear-piercing screech that shook every wall in The Laughing Loaf Bakery.

Maeve, my Irish breadmaker-in-training, groaned as she pulled pans of fragrant, buttery brioche out of our new oven.

"I'll be hearing power drills in my nightmares after this."

The back room where my staff and I were prepping and baking wasn't being renovated, but the pounding and drilling twenty feet away at the front of the store was hard to tune out.

Our remodeling had started two months ago, and since then we'd continued to use our back room to bake, while we served and sold baked goods at our popup location—a canopy five blocks away on a large greenspace.

Our remodel would update our space and allow us to serve lunch for the first time. I couldn't wait until the front counter and dining area of The Laughing Loaf finally looked like the drawings I'd signed off on.

Rose, my newest employee, looked up from the tart dough she was rolling out on the metal table. "Beck, can you teach me how to make beignets? I miss them so much."

"Everyone's been asking about them at the popup." Beck Rodriguez sliced apples on the cutting board. "We can't keep the beignets warm and fresh out there, so people will be very excited to see them when we reopen. They're going to sell out *fast*. I'd be happy to teach you, Rose. I'll need the help in the mornings."

As my bakery business grew, things were changing. Beck, who'd been my assistant for the past two years, would now manage our baking room, supervising our assistant bread baker, Maeve Killoran, and Rose Wilkins, our latest hire.

After Rose proved herself as a go-between for the popup and the Laughing Loaf's back room, I'd offered her a permanent job, so when we were back in the reopened bakery, she'd make drinks at the espresso machine and help with baking when needed.

With one more pair of hands helping, our prep sped up. In twenty minutes, we breathed a sigh of relief as we finished our day without construction noise. The air smelled of brioche, apple tarts, and cinnamon—mingled with the fragrance of sawdust, grout, and freshly varnished wood.

It was actually a pleasant smell. It was the smell of excitement. Of a new future for The Laughing Loaf Bakery.

In two weeks, as long as we didn't have any more delays, The Laughing Loaf would reopen, as a bakery and a restaurant serving lunch. We'd just hired three new employees—two River Grove High alumni, Tyler McCrae and Elise Delgado, and an older woman, Barb D'Amato—to work the counter, making sandwiches and wraps. The three were coming to the back room at 4:30 p.m. today for a short orientation.

For the past two days, before I started my prep in the back room, I'd carried my coffee into our new, enlarged dining area to take a seat at one of our new burnished wood tables. I was watching my dream come to life. The new floor was smooth, with natural hardwood planks, and the walls were painted a light tan, soon to feature some of my boyfriend Nate's gorgeous photos of local birds. I'd also found old photos from River Grove's history and had them reproduced for framing.

The dining area's new modern, curved wood chairs and tables looked like redwood, an homage to the town's history as a redwood logging center in Northern California's Santa Cruz Mountains. The curved white counter added the modern touch, looking sleek and hip under new pendant lights—Edison bulbs encased in what looked like sleek glass jars.

We had only two more weeks of running the Laughing Loaf popup bakery in the greenspace in front of The Riverside Saloon. Our baked-goods-filled tent had caught on, big time. With the warm weather and the outdoor beauty of late spring and summer, May had been the perfect time to launch it. River Grovians came out in force to mingle on the lawn and chat over coffee and pastries.

On the weekend, families laid out blankets and enjoyed breakfast while their children played on the lawn. Watching them made me love my quirky little town even more. When I moved here with my retired professor father and my little dog Biga, the town had welcomed me and my bakery warmly. I'd lived in an urban area in Seattle, so it had taken me a while to get used to some of the quaint small-town traditions—and the fact that everyone knew everybody's business.

Now I felt as much a part of this town as the people who'd grown up here. If River Grove was ever threatened, I rose to its defense. I had worked to uncover the culprits behind several crimes, alongside Police Chief Dave Westerman and Mayor Corinne Webster. Though my relationships with those two did not always go smoothly.

I glanced at the clock. In fifteen minutes, our three new hires would be here for orientation. Beck would sit them down at the worktables and give them an introduction to the bakery and how we were planning to operate our new lunch service.

Beck and Rose were sliding trays of tarts into the fridge for baking tomorrow morning. Maeve had just pulled a dozen brioche loaves out of the oven. They were cooling on racks, wafting their sweet, buttery smell throughout the back room.

At 4:30 p.m., the three hires showed up promptly at the back door. Beck greeted them and directed them to their seats.

She grinned with her usual cheeriness, her hands clasped together as if she couldn't contain her excitement. And I knew she really was that excited.

If she had any nervousness about her first duties as baking room manager, you wouldn't know it.

"Tyler and Elise, welcome!" College student Tyler had his wavy red hair tied back in a ponytail. Elise, daughter of the owners of River Grove's corner store, was petite and a little shy. But Beck and I had learned in interviews that she picked up things fast. Our third hire was Barb D'Amato, a River Grove native who'd run her own food imports shop until recently.

"Barb, it is *so* good to see you again," Beck said with a smile. The three hires had started chatting among themselves, so Beck waited for a minute or two.

"Take your seats around the metal table next to the bread racks."

Barb, a stocky woman in her fifties with salt-and-pepper curly hair, let out a deep chuckle as she settled on a stool near the racks. She wore a bright yellow and red Hawaiian shirt, emblazoned with male hula dancers. "My dears, this is pure torture, making us sit here next to this bread."

Maeve snorted from where she was mixing a batch of sourdough at the stand mixer. "That is your first test as a new employee, Barb," she said snarkily in her brogue. "If you can sit next to them without stealing a bite, you pass."

Barb laughed heartily and mimicked checking to see if anyone was looking then reaching for a loaf.

Beck sat up on her stool and turned to face the new employees, her dark brown eyes shining. She'd come a long way from the 22-year-old I'd originally hired. She was now The Laughing Loaf's secret weapon. Her cheeriness and genuine love for our customers brought them back. The pastries she crafted, like our beignets, became bestsellers on our menu.

"There are a few things to tell you about. The best place to park is in the alley behind us. There are always spaces there." She gestured to the open supply room door. "We have lockers now for your belongings in the supply room. Set up your combination today and *please* don't forget it. Also, it gets crowded in the back room and we get super busy, running back and forth in this space—so try to stay out of this room." She gestured to the industrial fridge. "Lunch is always on us while you're working, but please keep anything you bring for yourself on the bottom level of the fridge—the employee shelf." Beck giggled. "If you put it on any other shelf, we might end up making a sandwich out of it."

Now that the renovation crew had left for the day, Beck led the new hires into the front area to show them the long curved white countertop. I followed them and watched as Beck showed them the sink behind the counter, then the spots where the small fridge and the convection oven would be installed. Tyler had worked in a sandwich shop in Santa Cruz, so he nodded and told Beck it looked a lot like the setup at his previous job.

"And anything else will be in the industrial fridge in the back room, right?" Elise, a petite young woman with wide brown eyes, asked.

"Yes, if you're going back, give a shoutout to your crew mates to see if they need anything, to keep things running smoothly," Beck nodded.

"What if a customer wants a coffee drink with their meal?" Barb asked, eyeing the Italian espresso machine at the end of the counter.

"If you're working the lunch counter, you won't have to worry about that," Beck said excitedly. "The order will go to a display screen next to the espresso machine, so whoever's manning it will start on it right away."

We were automating our ordering system along with the renovation. It would be efficient and state of the art, but part of me would miss the simple fun of calling out the order to Beck, who'd worked the espresso machine from the start at The Laughing Loaf. We were serving more people and drawing customers in from Santa Cruz as well as Los Gatos and San Jose on the weekends. We needed to prepare orders quickly and make sure the meal and coffee got to the customer while they were hot and fresh.

Beck thought for a moment. She turned to me.

"Gracie, could you bring out a loaf of brioche and some butter? And a cutting board, a bread knife, a butter knife, and some plates."

Beck had mentioned wanting to try this as a group activity. I nodded and went to fetch these from the back room. When I came back, Rose had turned on the espresso machine.

Beck leaned against the counter, facing our new hires. "Our ordering system isn't up and running yet and our counter isn't ready for business, but how about we try a practice run-through with a customer. There'll be a treat in it for you." She smiled mischievously, then turned to me. "Rose, could you be ready for drink orders? And Gracie, I'd like you to be our first customer."

Rose took her place at the espresso machine, and I went around to the other side of the counter, playing the part. I looked around the dining area and the menu board, as if I'd just stumbled upon this new bakery and was trying to figure out what sounded good for lunch.

"Hmm." I tapped my lips. "Brioche? Maybe with some butter. And can I have an Americano with a splash of oat milk?"

The three new hires looked at each other and shrugged.

"Sure, why not?" Tyler grinned. He sliced the brioche and plated a piece, then Barb cut the butter and topped the bread with two pats.

"Oooh. The bread's still warm, too," Barb said with a shiver of delight.

Elise took the plate and set it down on the counter in front of me with an earnest look.

"Here you go, ma'am. Your coffee will be up in just a minute."

Not long after, 21-year-old Rose set a coffee cup on the counter with a bright smile.

"And here you go, ma'am."

What's with the ma'am? How old do I look?

"Well done, team," I said as I prepared to take a bite of my bread. I hadn't eaten lunch, and my stomach was growling in anticipation.

"Go ahead and make some for yourselves," Beck said. Tyler, Barb, and Elise made up plates with buttered brioche slices for everyone.

"Anyone want a coffee drink? Give me your orders!" Rose called from the espresso machine.

In ten minutes, the seven of us were gathered around the large oval table in the almost-finished dining area, brioche long devoured. We talked as we sipped our coffee.

"I worked at Suki's Sammie's in Aptos for two years. But now that I'm taking classes at San Jose State, this works better. The Laughing Loaf is on my way to school."

"You ran your own business, didn't you, Barb?" Rose pulled up a chair next to the woman.

"Sure did, hon." Barb sat back in her chair and nodded her head with a sad smile. "For fifteen years. Mangia Mama in Boulder Creek. An Italian food imports shop. We were doing great business. Then the new landlord hiked up the rent, and I didn't have any choice but to shut down last year. Everything not perishable is still in boxes in my garage here in River Grove. I grew up in this town. I'm a River Grove native. So, when I saw you were looking for help here, and you were serving food—well, it sounded like fun. Figure I'd work here and see where it led. Being around young people like you all makes me feel good."

I wondered how Barb was going to live on her paycheck from the Laughing Loaf. We paid a higher wage than most businesses in the area, but it wasn't going to help much with things like her mortgage or getting her on her feet again after her business closure.

"You're so down-to-earth and fun, Barb," Maeve said admiringly. "I'm sure you'll get through this time and get your business back on track."

Barb patted Maeve's hand across the table. "That's kind of you. I sure hope so. My husband Rocco used to tell everyone, if there's a way out of a hard spot, my Barb's gonna find it."

We talked and laughed together until I realized it was almost 5:30 p.m. and federal marshals Jeremy LaValle and Maura Piccelli were coming to meet with my father and me at 7 p.m. I had to run home and clean up first.

We said goodbye to our new hires after finishing up our conversations.

"So, we'll see you all for your first training at the counter a week from next Sunday—unless you hear from us that there's a delay." I looked around the table. "We'll keep you posted."

The new hires continued talking and laughing in the parking lot for a while. As Beck, Maeve, Rose, and I prepared to leave, I finally heard their cars starting up in the alley.

"What a great group to work with," Beck said with a sigh. "At first, I thought I'd be sad to leave the popup. Now I can't wait till we reopen."

It did seem like we'd hired a good team to run our lunch service. They seemed hardworking, experienced in customer service, and easy to get along with—even fun.

Yet there was a heavy feeling in the back of my mind after our time together. A premonition that, despite the opening of my beautiful new bakery, something was about to go horribly wrong.

I couldn't think of what it was. I put it down to the news that the federal agents would share with my father and me tonight.

There was a new threat to our peaceful life in River Grove.

All of it could be traced back to my ex-husband Ben, who'd been arrested for selling defense secrets to foreign governments--after I'd turned him in to the FBI back in Seattle.

It had only been a little over two years ago that witness protection had relocated us to River Grove.

I felt so comfortable here, it seemed like we'd lived here forever.

I didn't want anything to change that.

Chapter Two

My chihuahua mix, Biga, had stayed home with my dad again that day, so when I opened the front door, he tackled my legs as soon as I got inside.

"Biga boy. I missed you, too."

I bent down to pick him up. He nuzzled my face and started licking flour off my shirt. If there was any form of food within range, Biga sniffed it out and plotted how to get at it. Or convinced someone to give it to him.

My father, Dr. John Markley, a retired Physics professor, was finishing up making dinner in the kitchen. It smelled very enticing. He'd set the dining room table for us.

"Chicken stir fry and rice will be ready in about ten minutes, dear." My father had upped his game as far as cooking was concerned, thanks to me and his girlfriend Mary Jo teaching him some basic cooking techniques. I could now count on him making dinner for us three times a week. Granted it was usually something influenced by his dislike for spices, but I could always add those myself and at least I didn't have to make it.

To my surprise he set down a small bowl of chopped cilantro next to my plate.

"You know my feelings about the stuff," he said, his face contorting as he held the bowl far from his face. Some people are genetically wired to dislike the leafy green herb, and my father was one of them. "When I eat it, it tastes like soap. But I know you love it, dear." He gave me a sheepish look and turned pink. "And Mary Jo does, too."

"Thanks, Dad," I smiled. I wondered if Mary Jo had made it clear to him that having the herb on her table was non-negotiable.

Under the table, I felt Biga bump into my foot. He was jonesing for some dropped food.

I bent down to look at him and hissed. "You have your own food, Biga. It's in your bowl."

"How are you feeling about Jeremy and Maura's visit tonight?" I asked once I'd thrown Biga's chew toy back into the living room to distract him. I felt my stomach lurch as I thought about it. I wanted to know how much of a threat these dissidents actually were.

Agent Maura Piccelli had taken me aside at the debut of our popup in the Riverside greenspace last month. She told me they'd received intelligence reports of a dissident group in the Balkans called SABRE. They were trying to track me down for info on an oil pipeline. Ben had sold SABRE the shutdown codes and a list of the system's vulnerabilities. But he'd been arrested before he could hand them over.

It was reminding me of what had happened back in October when Russian spies paid me a visit, looking for schematics for a fighter jet. Ben had told his contacts that I would have the plans, since I had been in on the defense-selling secret scheme *with* him. I had nothing to do with Ben's spy dealings—and the FBI knew that.

It had taken Maura and Jeremy several weeks to meet with us about these Balkan dissidents. That made me wonder if the urgency of the threat had gone down a notch or two.

My father finished a mouthful of food and wiped his mouth. "I don't know what to think. The agents don't seem as concerned about this one. Perhaps the threat has passed."

I dug into my stir fry. I realized my dad, as usual, had gone *very* light on the spice. I went to the fridge to get some chili onion flakes, then ended up dumping most of the bowl of cilantro onto my food.

"Dad, they wouldn't come out here to talk to us unless there was still a credible threat. They're overworked as it is, and we're low down on their list."

As people in the WITSEC program, my father and I were unusual. We were part of the five percent of those in the program who hadn't actually committed a crime. After Ben was convicted in federal court, it became obvious to the foreign governments he'd worked with that I'd shut down their flow of secrets. I needed relocation, protection, and a new identity. Since my father had agreed to come into witness protection with me, his only child, he did, too.

"Seattle seems such a long time ago." My father said, taking a sip of white wine. He frowned. "Hard to believe we're still dealing with Ben's mistakes."

I couldn't think of Ben without feeling an undercurrent of anger, though those feelings had faded somewhat. Our life here was good.

Apart from the occasional murder, our new hometown had been a sweet, safe place to land after my ex-husband's arrest and trial. My dad and I both found friends, meaningful work, and even romance.

This new threat to our life here—whatever level it turned out to be—was disturbing.

After dinner, I loaded the dishwasher, wiped down the kitchen, and tidied the living room. I threw my clothes and a load of Laughing Loaf aprons into the wash. Then I sat down on the couch with my laptop, Biga curled at my feet, and did a quick check on Laughing Loaf's revenue for the month. The popup and the good weather had given our sales a nice bump.

I set out a plate of apple streusel muffins from today's bake on my father's desk, making sure to pull my dad's chair away from the desk so Biga couldn't use it as a stepping stone to get to the muffins.

At 7 p.m., I heard a knock on the door. With a quick look out the peephole, I saw Jeremy LaValle and Maura Piccelli on our doorstep, wearing their River Grove attire, which wouldn't call attention to themselves like their usual navy-blue suits.

"Gracie, good evening," Jeremy nodded. He was wearing jeans, work boots, and a black t-shirt with a picture of Johnny Cash bent over a guitar. Jeremy's wavy hair was cut very short, a giveaway that he might be in government or law enforcement, but he'd let his facial hair grow out into stubble. The look was convincing enough.

Maura dark eyes flitted back and forth as she stepped in and scanned the room. She wore a frilly lace top under a pale pink hoodie.

My father came out of his study dressed in a polo shirt and khakis—casual wear for him. He looked more jovial than I felt.

"Hello, John." Jeremy LaValle reached out to shake his hand. "Good to see you even under the circumstances. How is teaching going at the high school?"

My father smiled softly. "I'm actually tutoring the students. And really enjoying it."

"We'll need to meet in your study, John," Maura said curtly. "No windows and it's well insulated."

I'd brought in chairs last night in anticipation of this. We settled in next to my dad's desk in the small room, lined with bookshelves and smelling musty like an old library.

"So, you're both doing well," Maura began perfunctorily, not looking at us, but glancing at a notepad where she'd written some notes. Maura wasn't a small-talk person, but at least she tried.

"Gracie, you're set to reopen the bakery soon. And you've hired new staff for your expansion."

I hadn't told her, so I wondered where she'd heard about this. I knew there was a local operative who worked for the federal marshals, keeping an eye out for us in River Grove.

Back in October, that mysterious local contact, whoever it was, had saved our lives when the spies had come to our house to try to find the fighter plane schematic. The agents said they still weren't at liberty to tell us who this person was.

For a while, it had driven me crazy. Was it someone I knew? Maybe it was someone I saw every day. I'd certainly poked around to try to get info.

"It's going well," I said with a nervous smile. "We've got a good team. I'm excited to start serving lunch."

"Gracie, John—you made it clear to us last fall that you wanted to stay in River Grove." Jeremy looked at us both directly. "We offered to relocate you because of the threat from the spies, but you both told us you wanted to stay in River Grove. Your location is known by at least one foreign government, and that puts you at risk."

Maura gave us a sharp, probing look. "Are you still committed to staying here despite the risks?"

My dad and I didn't need to confer on this. We nodded.

"We are," my dad said.

"We'll see how you feel after we tell you what we've been hearing on the intelligence channels," Maura said, the firmness in her voice at odds with her pre-teen-girl pink ensemble. "You may want to keep your options open."

At her words, a pit opened up in my stomach.

"SABRE, a dissident political organization in the small monarchy of Satrovania, is looking to shut down an oil pipeline in the Balkans." Maura said in a low voice. "They're doing this to bring attention to their cause. This would be catastrophic, of course, and cause instability in the region. Your husband—"

"My *ex*-husband," I corrected.

"Ben Morrison found the codes to shut down that pipeline and he took payment from SABRE. But he was arrested before he could hand over the codes."

Jeremy nodded and continued. "Then Kyle Burnett, who wasn't arrested till a week later, spread the rumor that Gracie had the codes in her possession. SABRE came after Kyle to get them, but apparently, he never had them."

Déjà vu. I felt sick to my stomach as I listened to the events from our recent past. Ben had been furious when I'd turned him in. He'd retaliated in any way he could. And it had worked. Pointing the finger at me, his supposed accomplice, had continued to put me and my dad in danger.

Maura raised an eyebrow. "SABRE has been trying to bring down this pipeline for the past few years, and they've been unsuccessful. This is their one last chance—a desperation move for them. But there is some good news."

I sighed wearily. "Okay. What's the good news?"

Maura pressed her lips together. "I'm actually a little surprised by this. They don't seem to know your location. Their inquiries have been focused almost entirely on the Pacific Northwest. And oddly, Alabama—where we were planning on relocating you back in October. Which is concerning because that means there could be a leak somewhere on *our* side."

"Well, if they don't know where we are." My dad sat up in his office chair, looking relieved. "Then we could be fine after all."

My face must have shown my skepticism. Jeremy gave me a grim nod.

"You would be right to expect that will change, Gracie. It's only a matter of time before they find out."

I closed my eyes to stop the tears. I was so tired of this— not knowing when new danger would crop up thanks to the dealings of my ex.

"It'll be important for both of you to stay in touch." Maura frowned and absentmindedly tucked a pink bra strap back into her frilly shirt. "You both have your burner phones handy, right?"

My dad and I looked at each other and nodded. "Keep them hidden but nearby. If you notice anything unusual, maybe an unfamiliar group of people coming through town. Or at the bakery. Or outside the house here—" Maura's expression was dark, and there was an urgency in her eyes. "Notify us immediately."

I looked over at my dad, who was starting to realize this was a serious situation. He smiled weakly.

We stood up, and Jeremy reached over to grab a muffin from the plate on the desk.

"These look amazing," he said with a smile. "Something new at the bakery?"

"Apple Streusel Muffins," I said, trying to keep my voice from sounding completely dead. "My assistant Beck created them."

"Tell her they're delicious," Jeremy said, as he devoured the muffin.

Maura walked out of the room with my dad, as she casually asked him about seeing the sights in London, where she was headed for vacation later in the summer.

She'd just told us we could be in serious danger. How could the agents suddenly switch to lighthearted conversation about food and tourist sites? I knew this was their job, but, hey—this was our *life*.

NATE CALLED an hour later that night, at exactly 9 p.m., like he always did—even though he was away on a photo shoot in Yosemite National Park. Hearing his deep, resonant voice over the phone made me feel so good. And a little tingly all over.

"I wish you were here with me," Nate said, longing in his voice. "It's stunning. Have you ever been to Yosemite?"

After moving to California, I'd been preoccupied with the bakery and fitting into our new town. I hadn't had a chance to go sightseeing. "It sounds like I need to." I laughed. "Why don't you send me some pictures so I can dream about it."

I didn't want to tell him dissidents were on my trail. I wanted to hear him talk about the cute owls he was photographing and the gorgeous waterfalls he'd hiked to. Which he did.

Even with my head filled with beautiful descriptions of rock formation and waterfalls, I didn't sleep well that night.

Eventually Biga got sick of my tossing and turning and jumped off the bed.

I heard the thump of his paws dropping to the hardwood floor.

He'd deserted me.

Chapter Three

The next week passed by in a blur.

With sunny weather and mild temperatures, we did a great business at the popup.

The beautiful outdoor setting had changed things. It wasn't like people ran up to the popup in the morning to get their coffee and muffin and dash off for work. Customers took their time at the tables, leisurely chatted with each other, and sipped their coffee while enjoying the coolest part of the summer day.

As we got into August, it would get hot in the mountains. It was probably good that our time at the popup was coming to an end. Lunchtime and early afternoon would be best spent in the air-conditioned dining area back at the bakery.

One morning, Police Chief Westerman and Corinne Webster--aka Mayor C--came up to order their usual.

"Everything on schedule for your reopening?" Mayor C asked as I handed her coffee with oat milk and a kale frittata.

"So far. We've hired a lunch crew—and the front area's

coming along nicely. Just know you'll need to pin down a new morning meeting table. The dining area setup's changed a little."

The chief and the mayor had come into The Laughing Loaf every weekday morning to meet about River Grove public safety at the corner table in our old dining area.

I handed the chief a cup of drip coffee and a plate with what he'd been eating for breakfast during our time in the popup: a slice of Laughing Loaf sourdough spread with peanut butter. Last year, his doctor had told him he needed to cut out sweets, so we tried to accommodate him as best we could.

Mayor C and the chief lowered their voices as they talked excitedly about some new zoning measure the county was considering. Immersed in their own world, the two made their way slowly to an open bench with a view of the greenspace.

A few minutes later, I saw the chief's daughter, Renee Westerman, join them. The three chatted for a while, then Renee came over to order coffee.

"Gracie, good to see you." She was dressed a little too posh for River Grove and her big movie star sunglasses kicked that up a notch. "What do you have for pastries today? I'm hooked on those coconut lime scones. Any chance you've got some?"

"I'm making them back at the bakery, so we'll have them out here this afternoon. Stop by later if you're in town. Right now, we've just got cherry white chocolate."

"That's a little too decadent for me." She thought about it. "Oh, why the hell not. It's Friday, right?"

I laughed. "You got it. Treat yourself." I packed up a scone to go with her drip coffee. "Enjoy your Friday."

"I plan to," she said with a smile as she took her coffee and scone.

At 10 a.m., Rose came by with the cart, which was loaded with a full coffee Cambro and pastry-filled trays to replenish our breakfast items. It was warming up, and she was wearing cat-eyed sunglasses, a head scarf, a paisley camp shirt and a pair of bright red capri pants that looked like something a Hollywood starlet would wear in the 1950s.

"I love your look, Rose." I began pulling trays from the cart to restock the popup's display case with cinnamon rolls, scones, and muffins.

Rose's last job had been at a Santa Cruz thrift shop, and she'd taken full advantage of the employee discount to build her vintage clothing wardrobe.

"Thanks. This is one of my favorite outfits. It's supposed to hit 85 degrees today and I want to keep cool. I've been tracking steps on my phone. Did you know I'm doing about five miles a day between here and the bakery?"

"Not surprised at all," I said, looking out over the greenspace, where a mom and dad were playing with their toddler, all of them wearing shorts. "I wish I could put in that many steps." I handed a pile of napkins to a woman who'd come up to the popup after spilling coffee on her pants. "Anything happening at the bakery? Maeve said she might bring over some sourdough loaves later."

"She says she's planning on coming over after lunch."

Rose's face looked troubled. "Gracie, I think I should tell you this. Something a little strange happened at the bakery. Barb stopped by about an hour ago. I mean, I was loading up the cart near the baking racks, and I turned around and saw she was there. I hadn't even seen her come in. She was wandering around the back room, looking at stuff. I didn't even know she was there. She poked her head into the supply room, then I saw her standing by your computer, looking at things around your desk. Then she went to talk to Maeve at the mixer."

"Was she looking for me or Beck?" This sounded a little odd. "Why would she go to the bakery? She knows we're at the popup today."

Beck looked over at us with a thoughtful expression as she listened while arranging the new delivery of pastries in the display case. She'd been quieter than usual today.

"I told her that," Rose said. "She told me she might stop by and see you."

From what I knew of Barb, she was sociable and curious, and I got a sense she wasn't great at observing people's personal boundaries. Who knew what she wanted?

My first thought was she'd been offered a higher paying job somewhere else and came by to ask me if I'd pay her more.

"I'll talk to her," I said to Rose. "Thanks for letting me know." Rose tied up the full bag of trash in the popup's metal bin, hoisted it out, then put in a new bin liner. She gathered our empty trays and stacked them on the cart. "See you in a couple hours, Gracie. Ping me if you need anything." She smiled, put on her shades and rumbled the metal cart over the lawn to the sidewalk.

"That's really weird about Barb," Beck said, sliding the door of the display case closed. "But she doesn't have a lot to do right now until she starts work. Maybe she was just lonely."

"You could be right." Beck had insights about people that I didn't always pick up on—and she was also a nicer person than me. "Hey, by the way, how's the boss life? It's a big step for you, being in charge of the back room."

Beck smiled. "I'm a little scared about managing people, but I think I can do it. I know I'll have less time to be creative because I'm going to be busier." A shadow passed over her face for a few seconds. She looked like she was going to say something but then stopped.

"But I do have an idea for a summer treat," she said, brightening. "I've been playing with it at home. Sam really likes it."

"Always a good sign if Sam likes it. What is it?"

"It's a variation on what we already do. Strawberry shortbread tarts. It's getting warmer and I've been craving strawberries. Once we're back in the bakery, I'll make a batch. You can taste it and tell me what you think."

I smiled. "Beck, I can't think of a time when you created something that wasn't good." I gave her a pointed look. In the past two years Beck had grown more confident, but she had her moments of self-doubt. "Are you capable of making something that doesn't taste good?"

She turned pink and laughed sheepishly. "Gracie, you don't see *everything* I make." I never thought about that. I wondered if she'd been working on things she'd never showed me, things that didn't quite work out. All I'd seen was her long string of successes.

At 10:30 a.m., I looked around at the tables and benches, where customers lingered over their coffee. The chief called me a snoop, and I admit I was and still am. People fascinate me. I can't stop watching them.

The mayor and the chief sat at a nearby bench. The chief gestured as he explained something, while Mayor C nodded then leaned forward, her hand held up to interrupt.

Two women picked at the crumbs of their scones at one of the tables. By the tone of their voices, they were engaging in some juicy gossip. A group of teenagers threw a frisbee back and forth on the greenspace. One of them looked like Jeb Walker, who'd recently graduated from River Grove High, and was taking off for college back east at Princeton in the fall. I wondered if the group of frisbee players would stop by the popup for coffee drinks. I was missing our morning dose of high schoolers now that school was out.

By lunchtime, the greenspace had emptied out. The chief and Mayor C had left to go back to City Hall. The teenagers did end up heading in our direction, laughing and spinning the frisbee on their fingers while trying to pass it to each other.

As they came closer, I saw Jeb with someone I definitely recognized: Chief Westerman's granddaughter, Chloe, wearing her signature look: a torn black and red "punk" shirt, her blonde hair pulled back in a pony tail.

Yes, this was Chloe *"No, I Don't Like Jeb in that Way"* Westerman.

I'd asked her about him, since the two had studied together weekday mornings at The Laughing Loaf for most of spring semester.

As I watched—while trying not to look like I was watching—Jeb and Chloe left the group and walked over to a redwood tree at the edge of the greenspace. Then they looked around and realized there were people on the lawn. Chloe moved around to the side of the tree and laid back against it. Jeb put his hand on the tree above her and leaned in for a kiss. Chloe draped her arm languidly over Jeb's shoulder, and the two of them kissed in the shade, barely concealed from the rest of the people on the lawn. Good thing her grandfather was long gone.

Beck suddenly looked up from the display case.

"That's Chloe Westerman over there!"

I laughed. "I think it's better if we act like we've seen nothing."

"But I thought those two didn't get along. She said he was uptight. And a total nerd." Beck giggled. "They seem to be getting along very well now."

I watched the two of them until I realized I had to call Rose to bring back another Cambro of coffee and a thermos of oat milk if we were going to get through the next couple of hours.

I smiled as I pulled my attention back to my duties in the popup.

"They may learn the hard way that there's no keeping secrets in a small town."

Chapter Four

With the temperature rise in the afternoon, all our customers seemed to want was iced coffee.

And sweets.

I'd made up a batch of sourdough chocolate chip cookies first thing this morning, so I had Rose bring them over with the new coffee. The soft, creamy cookies sold out within the hour.

Reggie McFerrin, owner of The Riverside Saloon, came out of the music venue when word got around that we had them.

He made his way down the walkway, looking out of place on this sunny day when everyone else at the tables and benches was wearing summer clothes. He wore his usual black slacks, shirt, and blazer. As usual, I couldn't see his eyes behind his mirrored aviator sunglasses. I'm not sure I remembered what his actual eyes looked like; I think I'd only seen them once.

To anyone outside of River Grove, Reggie probably looked like a mortician or what I'd thought when I first met him—a vampire. In fact, Reggie, a former hippie who founded a commune here in the 1970s, had been mayor of River Grove four times. He was almost universally beloved in town. The Riverside Saloon brought people from all over the state to see concerts in almost every musical genre.

The corners of his mouth turned up in a smile. "Gracie, word has it you made your sourdough cookies."

I took out a small bag and stuffed it with two cookies from our dwindling supply, then passed it to him like I was making a drug sale.

"I wish I could give you more, but there's a run on them this afternoon."

He took his wallet out of his pocket.

"*Stop that.*" I put my hand up. "You gave us this tent and let us operate on The Riverside's greenspace." I scrambled for words. "Think of these cookies as...rent."

Reggie chuckled. He pulled up a chair and hung out at the popup while he ate his cookies and drank iced coffee. Even though we were on his property, I hadn't seen much of him since we'd been in the popup.

"You probably can't wait to be back in the bakery."

"I love being outdoors," I said with a sigh. "But the remodel's looking wonderful. It's set up so much better for us. And I can't wait till we're serving lunch."

"I'll have to come by and check it out, Gracie."

I'd felt a little odd about our lunch venture at first, since we would be competing against The Riverside for customers. Sort of, though the saloon didn't open for meals till later in the day. Reggie had never expressed anything but encouragement for The Laughing Loaf's plans.

Rose came by with the cart when we closed at 2 p.m., and she, Beck, and I loaded the remaining baked goods, the trays, and the Cambros onto the cart for our walk back to the bakery.

We were our own little parade as we rumbled down the street with our cart, waving at River Grovians.

"I miss being downtown at the bakery," Beck said sadly as she carried a box of napkins, forks, and coffee stirrers. "The popup's been so much fun. But the new bakery's going to be amazing. I can't wait till we're all working together." Beck's face looked beatific as she thought about next week's opening. "I have this feeling. I just know we're all going to be really good friends."

As we made our way down the street, that strange sense of impending disaster came over me again.

My assistant manager was right about many things.

I wasn't sure I agreed with her on this one.

WHEN WE CAME in the back door of the bakery, Maeve was wrapping sourdough loaves for overnight cold proofing. Since the workers were still drilling and sanding in the front area, Maeve had put on headphones and was listening to music, judging by the fact that she was singing along at the top of her lungs. Since it was Maeve, her voice was high and very much off key.

She didn't notice us come in until she went over to the oven to set up the next bake. She pulled the headphones off and set them on the table, laughing.

"Whoa, you're back." She continued wrapping the last tray of loaves. "I was enjoying making as much noise as the guys in the front area."

"So we *heard*," Beck said with a teasing smile.

I set out the leftover pastries on the wooden table and declared them up for grabs. Then Beck, Rose, and I got to work on our prep. I mixed cinnamon roll dough—less than I usually did, since tomorrow would be a hot day and cinnamon rolls were cold weather items. Then I pulled out the whole wheat loaves from the proofer. They were now at the end of their cycle, and I wanted to score a leaf design on their tops. Scoring was one of my favorite ways to add a finishing touch to my bread. The scorer (called a *lame*, pronounced *lahm*) held a razor blade. It took just a few strokes to create a simple design on a loaf.

Beck put on music and had to turn up the volume a little higher since the workers were using a drill on the cabinets in the front area.

"Hey, Rose?" I called to the young woman. "Can you check my desk for my bread scorer? I think I left it there this morning before we went over to the popup."

"Sure thing!" Rose went over to my office, which was basically a converted walk-in storage closet off the back room, left over from the days when this had been a bank building. It had just enough room for a desk with my computer and a few shelves in the back. I had a box of things I'd taken off the walls by the counter area when we started the remodel. I looked over to see Rose picking up papers and sorting through them.

"I'm not seeing it." She called out. "Oh wait, how funny. It's sitting here on the back of your desk."

On the back of my desk? I would never have left it there.

But there was something else I kept at the back of my desk. The key to a compartment that I alone knew about.

It held my burner phone for communicating with the federal agents.

Chapter Five

I took a deep breath, trying to stay calm.

I glanced around the desk to see if anything else was missing or out of place.

Rose brought back the scorer.

"Here you go, Gracie."

I thanked her with what I hoped was a casual smile.

Maybe I was on edge because of our conversation with Maura and Jeremy. Satrovanian dissidents might or might not be in the process of figuring out my location.

But one thing I knew for sure. Barb D'Amato had been in the back room today, and Rose said she'd been looking at things on my desk.

I didn't want to panic. I didn't want to make a big deal about something that my staff didn't know about and wouldn't understand.

I couldn't tell them I was in witness protection, and I certainly wasn't going to call an all-hands meeting to tell them--oh, by the way--dissidents looking for oil pipeline access codes might be stopping by the bakery soon.

I thought about my options while I plunged my hands

into the vat of cinnamon roll dough. Just as it always had, kneading the dough by hand felt calming; it centered me.

I'd wait till Rose left, and then I'd casually ask Maeve about Barb's visit to the back room.

After Rose took off for the day, I went over to the new combi oven where Maeve was setting up a bake for sourdough loaves on the display.

"So Barb came in today to visit, while we were over at the popup," I asked. "Did she say what she wanted?"

Maeve frowned. "She did say she was hoping to talk to you. Is that a problem?"

I studied Maeve's face. "No, I'd be happy to talk to her, but I'm surprised she didn't come over to the popup. She knew I'd be there."

Maeve shrugged as she watched the numbers go up on the oven display. "I mean, we hired her, right? She's an employee and this is her workplace. She can be here in the back room."

Maeve really liked Barb and was going to defend her, and I knew that. There was an edge to her voice.

"She hasn't started yet. Beck told the new hires that they needed to steer clear of the back room, since it's crowded and we're all working here. I'd like to make sure we're not having people wander into our workspace. It's a good idea to be careful, that's all."

Maeve gave me an odd look, but I smiled back.

"We're becoming a bigger operation. We'll have a lot more traffic coming through this room. I want to set some boundaries."

Beck raised her head from the pan of tart shells she was working on.

"Gracie's right. We told the new hires. When we're back here, there will be four of us in this space and three people up front who'll come back to get things. It's going to get busy."

Maeve thought about this. "Okay, I get that. But you're acting like Barb did something wrong. Barb's a sweetheart. She stayed and chatted with me a bit. She's harmless."

Again, I smiled and nodded. "You're right, Maeve. I just want us to be careful. I'll reach out to Barb and see what she wanted."

Maeve went to take loaf pans out for baking, while I pulled ingredients out for making more chocolate chip sourdough cookies, seeing how popular they were today. I dipped a measuring cup into our vat of sourdough starter and pulled out a gooey, bubbly mass.

After the construction workers left, the three of us worked quietly together, finishing up our respective preps for tomorrow. Beck's tart shells lay on the counter, ready to be filled tomorrow morning. The whole wheat loaves cooled on the baking racks, filling the room with a nutty, grainy aroma.

Maybe it was because quiet was such a rare thing during the renovation, but we didn't turn on any music. Beck, Maeve, and I kept to ourselves, working quietly and efficiently.

As Maeve worked, tight-lipped and unusually quiet, I wondered. How much of my concern about Barb was due to my fear of the dissidents finding me?

When I thought about it, the idea of middle-aged, Hawaiian-shirt-wearing Barb being in league with dissidents was pretty ridiculous.

Maeve left shortly before 5 p.m. to meet up with her boyfriend, Rafal. He was spending the night in River Grove at Mayor C's house, where Maeve lived during the week. The two of them were having dinner at The Riverside.

Before Beck and I closed down the bakery at 5 p.m., we went in to take a peek at the front area and counter.

The counter was polished and complete, and its surface shone, reflecting the glow of the new hanging lights above it. The front wooden base of the counter curved in an elegant s-shape, flowing under the sleek counter like a wave at the beach in nearby Santa Cruz. Workers had put a seal on the wood base today, hence the strong smell. The wood was the same color as the burnished wood chairs—a reddish brown, rich and glowing.

"It makes me want to cry, Gracie," my emotional assistant manager said softly, a look of awe in her brown eyes. "I loved this place before. Even when there hadn't been that much changed from the old bank building and the hamburger place. But this gives the bakery a whole new look. There's no place in River Grove like this. It's beautiful."

"I'm very happy with how it's turning out," I said as I stepped back from it to take the whole counter area in. "And so far, no more delays. I'm confident in saying we'll open Monday."

Beck turned to me, and her eyes searched my face. "You seemed like you've been worried about something today, Gracie. Were you afraid there'd be another delay? Like when they found mold in the restroom walls last month?"

What could I say?

"Now that we're getting right down to the end, it scares me." I wasn't lying here—this was true. "Like what's going to go wrong that we're not expecting." Like SABRE coming into my bakery, demanding that I give them access codes to a pipeline.

Beck was an optimist, through and through. Her philosophy was to assume that everything was going to work out.

And if it didn't, you made the best of it, rethought things, then picked yourself up and carried on.

"Maybe something will." Beck shrugged. "But we're almost ready to open—so it probably won't. The bakery's still going to reopen, even if it's a week or two later than we planned. And it already looks better than anything else in town. Everyone's excited to see us reopen."

The worst thing I'd done in the beginning was to underestimate my assistant, think of her as a naïve small-town girl, who'd never toured the world, gone to college, or lived outside of this small town.

I learned since then.

Beck Rodriguez, with her offbeat creativity, kindness, and persistent optimism, was in my life, and in my bakery, for a reason.

The two of us looked at things very differently.

Somehow, that made things better.

Chapter Six

When I walked in the door of my house, it took Biga a full two seconds to attack my legs and begin pawing at me to pick him up.

"Biga boy!"

I set down my bags and scooped him up in my arms. I cuddled with him on the couch, rubbing his belly and then cradling him in my arms like a baby, which he accepted as completely normal.

Yes, this is what we do. I am her baby.

He looked up at me with his big brown eyes, his paws folded in front of him, docile and, for Biga, angelic.

He'd missed me bad.

Another reason I'd be glad to be back in the bakery: Biga would be in his space off the back room. I'd be able to see him whenever I had time and take him for walks during the day. I know he missed it, and I could tell he missed me.

Then I had the thought: I wanted to re-do, even just redecorate, Biga's room off the back room at the bakery. So that when we reopened on Monday, he'd have a new place to be, too.

"Gracie, I didn't hear you come in." My father came down the hall from his office. He was dressed awfully nicely for someone who was going to stay in for the night—a light cardigan over a short-sleeved buttoned-down shirt, pressed brown twill pants and well-polished leather shoes. He looked like he was about to get an auditorium of college freshmen really pumped up about the laws of thermo-dynamics.

I shot him a smile.

"Ooh, *someone's* going out."

"After dinner I'll be going over to Mary Jo's." His cheeks blushed as he said it. After a time of "wanting some space," my father had started spending more time with Mary Jo. They talked about some things, worked things out. As my father told me in his typically understated way, things seemed to be going "quite well."

"You two got anything exciting planned?" I asked.

"Movie night. Mary Jo's going to pop some popcorn and we're watching another rom com. She's just gotten her big screen TV installed."

"Nice. Well, enjoy." Gone were the days when my dad had spent evenings lounging in his recliner reading physics papers from old students. Between tutoring high schoolers and reconnecting with Mary Jo, he seemed happier.

After letting Biga down, I pulled dinner fixings out of the fridge and started heating up beans and shredded chicken for tacos. Biga followed me, sure he was going to get a handout or anything I might drop on the floor.

We sat down to dinner, and I poured a half a glass of Spanish Rioja for each of us. I took a sip of the deep, earthy red wine and closed my eyes in bliss.

"Have you thought any more about what Jeremy and Maura told us?" I asked my dad after polishing off a taco.

My dad took a sip of wine. "It reassured me that they haven't found us yet. Until Jeremy and Maura raise the alarm, I'm not going to worry too much about it."

I told him about Barb wandering around snooping in The Laughing Loaf back room. And how my bread scoring tool had been left on the back of my desk, right near the compartment holding the key to my burner phone.

My dad frowned. "Well, that's strange. You don't think Beck or Maeve could have moved it?"

"Only Maeve would have needed a scorer, for the sourdough loaves, and if she did, I can't see how she would have put it there."

Granted, I had jumped to a lot of conclusions when Rose found the misplaced tool. Something struck me for the first time. My scorer had a razor blade in it. A blade that would be handy for opening things, like mail or sealed documents and also might be useful for getting into locked compartments. If I went darker with my thoughts, it could be an effective, concealable weapon.

"Rose said she saw Barb in my office at my desk. When I asked Maeve about Barb being in the back room, she seemed defensive. She really likes Barb."

My dad used a knife to shepherd some stray taco filling onto his fork. "If we hadn't just heard about SABRE, would you have had the same reaction, dear?"

Probably not, and that was the truth. The news of the dissidents looking for me took me right back to my scary encounter with the Russian spies last fall.

I shrugged "It wasn't appropriate for Barb to be wandering around the back room by herself. But I might have been panicking."

I didn't want this to steal my joy away from our upcoming reopening. The bakery would be opening in just a few days, and we had three new employees who got along great with the rest of the staff. The Laughing Loaf would open to our eager town on Monday morning, looking stunning.

There would be opening day challenges because there always are. There were on The Laughing Loaf's opening day two-and-a-half years ago. I wanted to be ready for those, not obsessing about the misplacement of my scoring tool.

But I'd keep an eye on Barb, just to make sure.

After taking a sip, my dad looked over at me, a half-smile on his face.

"I heard some interesting news today from one of my tutorees."

I raised an eyebrow and smiled. "Do tell."

"Apparently, Jeb has a *girlfriend*."

I tried to keep from laughing. "Really now. Did he say who it is?"

"He didn't tell me, but I've done some detective work." He looked proud of himself. "You're not the only one who can do that, you know."

This was amusing. "And what did you find out?"

"Two of the River Grove High students I talked to say he's going out with Amelia Gruber, that young lady who sings the anthem so beautifully at the River Rats' softball games. Can you believe that?"

As I realized what had happened, I wanted to laugh. Chloe Westerman was smart. She was also good friends with Amelia. She and Jeb had almost blown it on the greenspace today, but she'd figured out a way to play the River Grove gossip machine.

And I'm sure Amelia had been in on it.

Clever girl.

After my father left for Mary Jo's, I lay down on the

couch with my laptop, Biga curled up at my feet. I did some online browsing to come up with things for Biga's room at The Laughing Loaf.

A new bed would be nice. And maybe some new toys. Biga loved anything that squeaked; maybe it activated some primal impulse in him to hunt small, squeaking creatures. If the toy was bacon-scented, that was a plus. I also found an interactive ball that would roll around and make a dog chase it. This would drive Biga crazy, but it would be hilarious to watch—so maybe more of a gift for me.

I turned the screen around to show Biga, who raised his head, then laid it back down on my foot, unimpressed.

I added a soft dog mat for inside his pen to the order, and found out all of these could be delivered overnight.

While it was still light outside, I took Biga out in the backyard. We had a long chase and play session around the yard, and I was able to get a few steps in myself.

Chapter Seven

With our reopening only three days away, Beck, Maeve, Rose and I sat down to finalize our bakes for reopening week.

The popup had been busy today. Before we opened, Beck and I hung a new sign I'd had made above the canopy opening. With the bright red color and big lettering, there was absolutely no way you could miss it. We'd been here at the greenspace for two months, and River Grovians tended to fall into habits easily.

I wanted to make sure *everyone* knew where to go for their coffee and pastries when we reopened.

The Laughing Loaf Bakery –
Reopening 7 a.m. Monday!

Then Beck had made a handwritten smaller sign to attach to it:

Say hello to your old friends...
Beignets, espresso drinks, and the Laughing
Loaf Joke of the Day!

We'd be re-introducing items we hadn't had in two months. And retiring some of the bakes that we'd used as specials just for the popup, like macarons and focaccia.

And really bad dad jokes would be back.

"I'm going to miss macarons," Beck said sadly. "But we could always bring them back another time of the year. We could make them in colors for certain holidays—ones in pastels for Easter, black and orange for Halloween." By the look on her face, she was already visualizing them.

"I vote to keep the apple streusel muffins." Rose sat up on her stool.

"Already on the list." I pointed to the menu draft and nodded. "They're a customer favorite now."

Beck took notes so we could put together a new schedule for what to prep and bake each morning. Rose would be helping Beck since she'd been inspired by her time in the back room and wanted to try baking. And since Maeve was still commuting back to Napa for her weekend job at Pain Parisienne, Rose agreed to work Saturdays alongside Beck as a beginning baker.

Later today, Maeve and I would put together a bread schedule. We'd need sandwich breads on hand—sourdough, whole wheat, and rye—and a flatbread for wraps and possibly flatbread pizza, as well as breadsticks to serve with soup.

"Rafal sent me a great flatbread recipe last night,"

Maeve said. "Seriously, it is *sooo* good. He's been making them at Pain Parisienne. It makes a killer wrap."

"Great. Let's look at that before you take off for the day."

When I got a break from prep, I went into my office. I checked that, yes, the key to my secret compartment was still there. When I opened the compartment, there was my burner phone. I slipped it into the inner pocket of my purse and zipped it up. Maybe I'd keep it there, or even at home, for a while.

I used my regular phone to call Barb. I thought I'd be blunt and just ask why she'd wanted to talk to me. If she had gotten some better offer, she probably would have gotten hold of me right away.

After four rings, Barb picked up.

"Barb, this is Gracie from The Laughing Loaf. Our baker, Maeve, said you stopped by the back room yesterday. She said you needed to talk to me."

There was a pause.

"Hi, there, Gracie." Her voice sounded hoarse. "Uh, yes. I wanted to ask you—uh, what time does the shift end on Monday?"

Hmmm. I'd heard Beck had mention this to the new hires at least twice. Then the handouts we'd given Tyler, Elise, and Barb had it printed prominently at the top, right above the job description.

How could she have possibly missed this?

"All your shifts start at 10 a.m. and end at 2:30 p.m., when the bakery closes."

"Got it. Thank you, Gracie. Guess my old lady brain got its wires crossed." She let out a hearty laugh.

Just from talking with her in the interviews, I knew Barb was sharper than this.

"No problem." My finger hovered over the hangup button as I saw Maeve pass by my office with an inquiring glance. "So, Barb, we'll see you Sunday for training at the counter—at 1 p.m."

I did not know what to make of Barb. Was it my paranoia that made me suspect she'd been nosing around my desk? Still, Rose said that's exactly what it looked like she was doing.

But *why* would she be doing that?

At 5 p.m., right after Beck and Rose left for the day, Maeve's boyfriend Rafal poked his dark curly head in the back door.

Rafal had taught Maeve to bake afterhours at their former employer in Napa, Night Rose bakery, owned by the horror-themed baker Daniel Bordelman, who had not treated Rafal, or any of his employees, well.

Rafal was thriving at his new employer, Pain Parisienne, and was developing a reputation as an innovative baker himself.

He looked so much happier and relaxed than when I'd seen him last. But then, the last time I'd seen him he was being interrogated as a suspect in his boss's murder.

"Gracie, I'd love to see your operation. Mind if I come in?"

I waved him in and wrapped him in a hug. "Of course." Maeve and I showed him around the back room and gave him a tour of the 99-percent-finished front counter and dining area. The small convection oven would arrive tomorrow, and an IT guy was coming to do a training with the ordering system, so we could learn it before we opened.

"Sunday we've got the lunch service crew coming in for training," I told him. "Then Monday's the big day."

Rafal looked around the front area and smiled softly. "This is perfect, Gracie. You've planned out the work area well. I wish we had all the space you have here. Hope opening day goes well for you."

"We'll be trying some new breads for sandwiches and wraps. Do you have anything you'd recommend? Maeve said you've got a great flatbread recipe."

"I'll email it," Rafal nodded. "This flatbread is soft and not too thick. We've been expanding our line of wraps. We've got the tourists coming in wanting something premade that still tastes fresh."

"It's delicious," Maeve said, smiling up at Rafal, and leaning into him affectionately. "Sometimes when we're working, we just tear off pieces to eat and smear them with butter."

After the two left to start their drive back to Napa for the weekend, I zested a bag of limes, then took out flour, butter, sugar, and eggs, and mixed a double batch of lime coconut scones. I rolled out the dough, laminated it with butter, folded it and turned it and then rolled it out again four times. The lime zest smelled heavenly. Nate loved the smell on my skin after I'd made these scones. It drove him a little crazy.

He wasn't due to get back from Yosemite till tomorrow afternoon at the earliest—and after he got home, we wouldn't have much time together with everything I had to do for reopening.

After I slid two trays of cut scones into the freezer, I went back to look at the job applications locked in a drawer in my desk.

I pulled out Barb's application and looked it over. Even

as I read it, I groaned at myself: *Why are you so suspicious of this woman?* Her references had checked out just fine. I'd even had a phone chat with her former assistant manager at Mangia Mama, and she said great things about her former boss.

Barb D'Amato was a graduate of River Grove High, had a year of community college, then worked at her brother's auto repair shop in Santa Cruz for five years. After marrying and having a daughter, she was out of the job market for ten years, then she started Mangia Mama. She'd run the Italian foods business out of her home then was able to set up shop in downtown Boulder Creek. Her former assistant manager, Carlene McCaffrey, had confirmed that Barb's landlord had sold the building. The new owner had raised the rent.

Barb seemed to be exactly who she said she was. And maybe the snoopiness was part of her personality.

Wasn't it a little hypocritical to slam her for something I liked to do myself?

Chapter Eight

I woke up Saturday morning when Biga poked his wet nose in my face. I turned my head over on the pillow.

"*Rude*, Biga."

Oh, geez.

I sat up.

My alarm hadn't gone off at 5, my weekend wakeup time. It was 5:45 a.m. Nate and I had talked for an hour and a half last night, and I'd gone to bed late.

I quickly rolled out of bed and nearly fell on the floor. Thankfully, it wouldn't take me long to get ready; I'd put clothes out last night. I got dressed and started up the coffeemaker in the kitchen to get my pre-coffee—which would give me a hit of caffeine to get me to work.

Biga gave me a cold look, then crossed the hall to scratch on my dad's door to let him in.

"Sorry, Biga boy. I gotta go. On Monday, you'll be back in your new, remodeled pen with me at the bakery. Aren't you excited?"

That did not placate him. He gave me some side-eye

then continued scratching at the door until my father let him in.

Beck was already there when I got to the bakery, mixing up a bowl of streusel topping for the apple muffins, while singing along to one of Maeve's 90s Brit Pop playlists.

Beck looked up, her eyes much more awake than mine. "Did you sleep in?"

I smirked. "Biga woke me up when my alarm didn't go off. Did you make coffee?"

"Of course," Beck said, still swaying to the music. "But when I'm done with this, I can make you a latte if you want, Gracie."

"Yes, *please*." I took the cinnamon roll dough out of the fridge and set it on the metal table to start rolling it out. "I'm still waking up. Nate and I stayed up talking too late last night."

"He gets back today, right?" Beck covered the bowl of streusel crumbles and went to wash her hands.

"Yes, and if he gets in early enough, he'll come out to the popup, since it's our last day. Mary Jo and my dad might stop by, too."

"Can you believe it?" Beck stopped and shook her head. "Our time at the greenspace has gone by so fast."

Beck went to the front area to make our lattes, while I started rolling out slabs of dough for cinnamon rolls. I mixed up the butter and brown sugar-cinnamon filling on the stove, then added a couple dollops of caramel sauce to the mix—my secret ingredient. It gave the mixture a dessert-ish flavor and the texture of sticky buns.

Cinnamon rolls were the staple of our bakery offerings. They were more popular in colder weather, but when we ran out, even on some of the hottest days, people would go away disappointed.

Beck set down my latte on the metal table. Within a few sips, I felt the pleasant jolt of caffeine in my system.

Rose came in the back door at 7 a.m., looking stylish in another vintage find—a navy-blue, bandana-print jumpsuit with spaghetti straps, covered by a cute, crocheted shrug. It looked too fancy for bakery work, but with an apron, she'd be fine. She was smart to dress for hot weather since she'd be working at the popup for part of the day.

"Hey, all." She stripped the shrug off and hung it up on a hanger on the rack, then slipped on a Laughing Loaf apron. She pulled her hair back into a low ponytail then slipped a hipster beanie over it to keep stray hairs out of the baking process.

"Beck's going to teach me how to make muffins and macarons today. I'm excited to start actually baking."

Beck took a gulp of her latte. "I'm glad you'll be able to help us on the weekends. You'll pick it up fine. The more you do it, the better you'll get. Learning how to bake will help you understand how everything else works around here."

By 7:30 a.m., despite my lateness, we had our main offerings baked and ready to take to the popup. Rose and I slid the wrapped trays onto the cart and lifted the coffee Cambro and milk ice chest up onto the top.

For the morning, Beck would go with me to the popup, and Rose would stay at the bakery, ready to load the cart up with more baked goods and coffee—and she'd work on a baking project Beck had set up for her. In the afternoon, when things were less busy at the popup, they'd switch places, and Rose would get a chance to sell baked goods and meet customers.

Beck and I pushed the cart out to the greenspace at what would be the coolest time of the day. A few people were out walking their dogs. One older lady with white hair and a tie-dyed dress was pushing a stroller. We peered into it, expecting to see the woman's cute, cuddly grandbaby. Instead, we were shocked to see a grey, furry rabbit inside . When the lady passed, we started laughing uncontrollably.

"I *thought* that was a really strange-looking baby," Beck said, amid giggles.

"Me, too. But what can you do?" I snorted. "There aren't a lot of great ways to take your rabbit for a walk."

The greenspace was quiet this early, except for the dog walkers and a group of older ladies doing slow, graceful tai chi movements in a shaded area near The Riverside. A light breeze ruffled the tops of trees that I suspected would go away when the afternoon heat hit. We rolled up to the popup and started unloading onto the table.

Beck had been having more quiet periods lately, and now she set about loading up the display case without conversation. I'd come to know that this meant Beck was in deep thinking mode.

"Everything okay, Beck?" I asked, as I set up the coffee Cambro and our insulated cooler of milks.

She swallowed and continued loading muffins into the case for a minute or two.

"Sam and I have been talking this week." She paused then looked up at me, as if to gauge my reaction. "About having a baby."

It startled me. I shouldn't have been surprised. Young adults who'd grown up in River Grove got married young and once they were financially established, started having families. Three of Beck's five older brothers had young kids. But I'd expected that Beck would stay for a few years in her position at the bakery before that happened. She loved her work. The Laughing Loaf was what it was because of Beck. It was hard to think of her switching gears to be a mom.

"How do you feel about it, Beck?"

She looked down at the table, a soft smile growing on her face. "I've always wanted kids. I just knew that's what I'd do. But now I'm doing something I love, something I think about all the time." She frowned. "Sam comes from a big family, too. He wants to start having kids, and he'd be a great dad."

I nodded. Sam was loving and thoughtful. If Beck had any hesitation about starting a family, he'd respect that.

Beck pulled a napkin from the box on the table and blotted her eyes. "I'm so scared, Gracie. I want to do both things."

I thought about this. "I'm not an expert at this, but I think you can."

She slid the display case closed and looked over at me, her brown eyes moist. "I don't want to end up doing a bad job with either one, you know?"

I pondered what to say to my assistant manager. I had friends in Seattle who had children and a career. It was hard to do both, but to be fair, their husbands worked long hours in the tech industry. These weren't Sam-quality husbands.

"You could work part time for a while. You could see how that works for you." I poured myself a cup of coffee from the Cambro and tipped in a dollop of oat milk. "Do you have any ideas about childcare?"

Beck brightened. "My mom. She watches my brothers' kids, and it works out really well."

Beck's mom scared me, with her straitlaced, slightly judgmental ways. At the same time, she'd raised Beck—and Beck was a wonderful person.

I smiled. "It sounds like you've thought this out. We can talk about how this would go with work when you get closer to this happening. You've got my support, Beck, no matter what you decide."

Beck burst into tears, just as a man came up with his dog to order. I hugged her and held her for a moment. I felt myself tearing up.

The man stood there awkwardly.

I turned and smiled to him. "Sorry, we were having a moment."

His look softened. "That's no problem. Take your time. When you're done with your moment, I'd love a cinnamon roll and coffee."

The rest of the morning, I thought about what Beck had told me. She'd been quieter this week, and I wondered if it was because she was feeling that conflict intensely at work —doing what she loved. I couldn't picture her giving up her work at The Laughing Loaf. I was trying to think of how we could work around her situation if she did decide to go the baby route. I'm sure we could, but we'd have to do some juggling. Either training our existing staff or hiring someone new.

I reminded myself this wasn't something I needed to deal with right now.

There were other things to deal with.

And they were coming at us fast.

SATURDAY HAD ALWAYS BEEN one of my favorite times at the bakery, and that had carried over to the popup. No one was in a hurry, and everyone seemed to be in a good mood.

As the sun rose higher in the sky, the greenspace filled up with families, who came over to the popup to get breakfast treats, then enjoy them at the tables or benches or on the grass. Tristan Conway, reigning champion of the River Grove Chili Cookoff, came up to the booth with his wife Kira and little boy Rowan, who pointed up to the display case excitedly with his usual, very sticky hands.

Sky Robbins, River Grove High School's recently graduated class clown, came up with his brother and mom to get scones and muffins.

"Hey, Sky, good to see you." I smiled, handing his mom a bag of breakfast pastries.

"Guess I can't get a cherry blossom latte here," he said glumly, his hands shoved in his shorts pockets.

"We can't do espresso drinks out here. You can get one next week, when we're back in the bakery."

The eighteen-year-old snapped his fingers and shook his head and proceeded to talk like the eighty-year-old man he often seemed to be on the inside. "Well, darn, Gracie. I was really looking forward to it. I'm working all next week at the Santa Cruz Boardwalk. Guess it'll have to wait."

"You're working at the Boardwalk?" I couldn't imagine a workplace more suited for Sky than the oceanside amusement park. "Where in the Boardwalk?"

"The Giant Dipper coaster," he said, his eyes lighting up for the first time. The Santa Cruz Boardwalk, eight miles away on the coast, was a good old-fashioned amusement park. The Giant Dipper had to be one of my favorite rides ever—a 100-year-old wooden coaster with an awesome dip and lots of creaking.

"Sky, that's awesome!" Beck turned around from the coffee Cambro. "Sam doesn't like thrill rides. Gracie, you and I need to go over and ride the coaster."

"I'm so up for that," I said, handing Sky his iced coffee.

"Nate's the same as Sam when it comes to rides. That's it. Beck, let's plan a field trip."

Sky and his family took their breakfast over to a bench, and we continued serving the long line of Saturday morning customers.

At 11:30 a.m., as we were preparing to head back to the bakery, my phone rang.

"Gracie, it's Rose," Rose said breathlessly. "*Okay.* So this is weird. I was working on the baking project Beck gave me—the beignet dough. I was heading for the fridge with it, when I looked up and suddenly there she was."

"Who? Who's there?" Though I had my suspicions.

"Barb. Here in the bakery. I'd locked the back door, too. She must have come in through the front where the tech guy is setting up the ordering system."

"Is she there now?"

"She just left. I told her we weren't allowing anyone in the bakery right now, and she needed to leave. She laughed and asked me what I was going to do about it. She said I wasn't her boss. I'm sure she was there for a few minutes before I noticed her. She was wandering around looking at things in the bakery. And she was in your office again. Sitting in front of your computer."

I didn't say a swear word, but I certainly thought one. What was this woman's problem? What was she after?

I worried about what she might have found. The burner phone was at home. My work computer was old, and I worried that I had information from my life in Seattle on it. Could Barb have been trying to find information on my past?

My heart pounding, I thanked Rose and hung up. Beck looked at me with concern, so I told her what Rose had said about Barb.

"I can't believe Barb talked that way to Rose." Beck looked indignant, an emotion I rarely saw on her face. "What are you going to do?"

"I'm going back to the bakery. Then I'm calling Barb. I want to make sure I'm there till we lock up tonight."

Beck manned the popup while I walked across the greenspace toward the highway and down to the alley way to The Laughing Loaf's back door.

I knocked on the back door. Looking very relieved, Rose let me in.

"No other sign of Barb?"

Rose shook her head. "She was parked in the back. After I asked her to leave, she stomped out and I saw her car pull out and take off down the alley."

"Thanks for keeping an eye on things, Rose. And for telling Barb she shouldn't be here."

Her blue eyes, carefully lined with black eyeliner, looked pained. "I'm so sorry I didn't know she was here, Gracie. It was like she was a ghost or something. She just materialized here in the back room and was going through your desk and nosing around. I asked the ordering software guy, and he said she just walked right past him. He assumed she worked here."

Well, she would as of tomorrow.

Or maybe not.

Rose had just brewed coffee and loaded it into a Cambro to take over. I helped her load the metal cart with trays of Beck's tarts, a box of macarons, and a sliced focaccia topped with cheese and vegetables.

"Have fun. Thanks for keeping an eye on things here, Rose."

After Rose was on her way out the door, I went up to

talk to the ordering software rep. He was preparing to leave for the day.

"Hi, Gracie—everything's installed. Ted will come by and do the order system training tomorrow for you and your employees at 2. Should be quick. Do you have any questions?"

"I appreciate getting the system up and running." I smiled. "I do have a question. There was a woman who would have come through the front door. About an hour ago. Curly hair, heavy set. Probably very talkative—"

"Oh, sure." He raised his eyebrows and laughed. "She chatted me up for about ten minutes. Told some funny stories and then asked about you and the bakery. I assumed she worked here, but I guess she wasn't supposed to be here, according to your baker in the back room."

"No, she wasn't."

"Sorry about that." He shrugged. "She came right in the door like she belonged here."

I nodded. "I can see where she would. You didn't know."

The man bent down to pack up his case. "Well, you're good." He nodded. "Your system's up and running. Looks like this was the last piece of the puzzle, huh?"

I looked around the gleaming front counter, now outfitted with new displays connected to the espresso machine and food prep stations. Shelves and racks were set up above the back counter, and the refrigerated case for sandwich items was up and running. The small refrigerator for milks was humming under the counter by the espresso machine, and the convection oven sat on the back marble counter, within easy reach of employees who needed to warm breads, buns, and pastries.

The furniture in the dining area looked perfect, though

I'd probably make some last-minute adjustments before Monday's opening.

"I think we're set now, apart from some wall decorations."

Beck and I would hang up framed photos of River Grove's history tomorrow, and I'd also set up Biga's pen off the back room with his new bed and toys.

After the system installer left, I walked around the front area, filled with awe at my new bakery.

I ran my hand down the smooth, cool counter, then walked around the dining area, taking in the smell of newly polished hardwood.

My delight was tarnished by my fears about what Barb had been up to in her snooping today and yesterday.

What was she after?

Had she found it?

Was she going to pass it on to someone else?

At the least, I needed to call her. Her refusal to follow our rules about staying out of the bakery back room, then her treatment of Rose, was enough for me.

Her services were no longer required.

Chapter Nine

First, I made sure the front and back doors to the bakery were locked. I went through the entire bakery, from the backroom to the front: both restrooms, Biga's room, the front counter, and the dining area.

I didn't want any ghostlike apparition of Barb hiding out or finding her way in. Barb had an uncanny ability to get into our bakery unseen.

It wasn't going to happen on my watch.

With a heavy sigh, I sat down at my desk, pulled out Barb's application and punched in her number.

The phone rang then rolled over to her message. At this point, the folksy cackle of Barb's voice made my stomach turn.

"Well, well, well. You've reached Barb D'Amato. Leave me a message and if you're lucky, I'll call you back, hon. *Ciao!*"

"Barb, this is Gracie Markley from The Laughing Loaf. Since you have shown an inability to abide by the rules

Beck set down in the employee orientation--*and* you showed disrespect to a bakery employee--we won't be moving ahead with your employment at the bakery. You'll receive a check for your hours in training and orientation. It'll be sent to your address on record."

I hung up, then slunk down in my chair. I pulled out my stack of "keepers" from the job application file—candidates we'd all felt pretty good about. I'd call them to see if we could get at least one of them in for tomorrow's lunch service training.

Barb could be harmless—just someone who liked to nose around in other people's business. Or she could be trying to get information on me to pass on to someone else. I wasn't just being paranoid: I knew from what the federal agents told me, there was a group of people out there trying to find me. Since she'd lost her business, Barb was in desperate need of money. What if someone paid her to verify I was the wife of Ben Morrison, notorious seller of defense secrets and keeper of the pipeline access codes?

Tonight, I'd talk to Jeremy and Maura.

Sitting around worrying about this wasn't going to get anything done. At the end of today, we'd take down the popup and bring everything back to the bakery. Tomorrow, Beck and I would hang pictures, stock shelves, and put the final touches on the bakery for Monday's opening.

And of course, train our lunch crew tomorrow afternoon.

While Beck and Rose worked at the popup, I turned on an '80s pop playlist and prepped several trays of scones for the freezer and mixed a batch of country sourdough—all for Monday's opening. Wham! played as George Michael sang, telling me sadly, that he was never going to dance again.

At 1:30 p.m., Beck called.

"Gracie, can you bring over a Cambro of coffee? And another tray of macarons and any sourdough starter chocolate chip cookies you have left. People are craving sweets, apparently."

"Sure, I'll be over in fifteen minutes."

My stomach was feeling nervous and uncertain. Preparing to head over to the greenspace kept my mind off today's incident with Barb.

I brewed a big batch of coffee in the commercial drip maker, then went in search of cookies. We had a tray of bright purple *ube* macarons and three dozen sourdough starter chocolate chip cookies, so I packaged these all up and set them on the rack by the back door, so I could load them into my car.

Then I hoisted the heavy drip carafe up and poured it into a clean Cambro. Loading up our daily deliveries to the popup was giving me muscles. Even though he beat me every time, I was at least able to put up some resistance to Nate when it came to our friendly arm-wrestling matches.

I heaved the Cambro down to the back step, then I turned the keys in the top and bottom locks on the door, to make sure no one could get in.

I loaded up and backed out of my spot in the alley parking. I noticed a familiar-looking car a few spaces down from where I'd parked. I thought I'd seen the car when we'd had the new hires in for training.

As my tires crunched over the gravel, I saw something brightly colored in the middle of the alley. I braked to avoid hitting it and the car lurched forward. I heard the load of trays and Cambro shift in my trunk.

It looked like somebody'd left a pile of clothes in the road.

"What the—" I turned off the car and got out to see what it was.

That's when I saw the cheery, brightly colored Hawaiian shirt.

On the lifeless body of Barb D'Amato.

Chapter Ten

I turned her body and took her pulse.

I felt nothing.

As I let go of her arm and Barb's body rolled onto her back, I saw the front of her shirt, soaked in blood. It looked like she'd been shot.

I tapped the chief's number on my phone.

"Chief, I just found a woman dead in the alley, right before it joins with Loudon Lane. She's actually one of my new hires."

"We'll be right there, Gracie," the chief said and hung up. It must have been a minute and a half later when the River Grove PD squad car pulled up from Loudon Lane and blocked the alley. I sighed with relief. I'd been afraid someone would turn into the alley and miss seeing the body until they hit it.

The chief and Brad Castro, his deputy, got out of the car and stooped down by the body. Brad took out his phone. I could hear him talking to a dispatcher.

The chief frowned as if he were trying to remember something then suddenly gave a nod. "She's a River Grove old-timer. Barb D'Amato." He pulled on gloves and turned the body gently. "She's been shot. Gracie, this close, you must have heard something."

"I had the music turned up loud," I said, swallowing. Guilt singed the corners of my thoughts. If I'd actually heard the shot, getting help could have saved her life. I'd been annoyed with Barb, but I certainly didn't want her dead.

"I'd just hired Barb for the lunch crew. She was going to start tomorrow. I wish I'd heard it and called 911. She might have lived."

"Not with this wound." The chief shook his head. "Somebody knew what they were doing, and they wanted her dead."

My thoughts raced. Had Barb been working with the SABRE, helping them find me? Maybe they'd gotten information confirming my whereabouts and didn't need her anymore.

Gracie, hellooo! This is not about you. Or this is probably *not about you. A woman you knew was shot and killed.*

I leaned back against my car. The trees behind the lot ruffled in the afternoon breeze. A siren wailed faintly in the distance, coming closer.

"When the EMTs get here, we need to ask you about what you saw, Gracie. You've talked and worked with Barb recently."

Sure, I could tell him. It would feel strange to do it, since my experience with Barb hadn't been positive.

I remembered what I'd told people about talking to the police in a case: tell them everything, even if you don't think it's important. You can't judge. What you might not think is important may be the piece of the puzzle that completes their understanding.

I stood up suddenly, remembering Beck and Rose over at the popup, waiting for coffee and cookies.

I texted them telling them there'd been an accident, and to stay put as best they could until we closed in an hour. I'd tell them details as soon as I could.

A text message popped up. Nate was driving back from Yosemite and almost back in River Grove.

> Just hit the Bay Area, love. See you at popup in an hour?

I gulped. With what had just happened, I'd forgotten he was meeting me there.

> There's been an accident. Come to the bakery.

The EMT van pulled up on Loudon Lane, right behind the RGPD squad car.

Now the icon with Nate's face appeared on my phone. He was calling, which I should have expected. I'm sure my text message sounded alarming.

"Gracie, you need to tell me what's going on."

"I found Barb, the woman we'd hired to work the lunch shift, dead in the alley." I told him about almost hitting her body as I headed out to the greenspace.

"So she was shot." He spoke quietly, his voice hoarse. "In River Grove."

"I'll tell you more when you get here. I have to talk to the chief now." The EMTs were with Barb's body. They covered her then gently lifted her onto a stretcher. They prepared to carry her to the open back of their van.

Nate was having a difficult time with my involvement in River Grove crime solving. He'd lost his family—first his parents in a plane crash, then his brother Nico, who was murdered here in River Grove two years ago.

"I'll see you at the bakery soon. Be careful, Gracie. Don't try to handle this yourself."

I hung up without promising anything. I wasn't sure who had killed Barb, and I had no idea whether it was related to the dissidents on my trail. Which...I had not told Nate about. Now that he was back from his shoot, I needed to fill him in.

Within ten minutes, the EMT van was gone. After I moved my car back to my parking spot, the chief approached me, his tablet in hand. Brad followed close behind. He'd gotten the call just after getting off duty at his other job at Best Buy, and he was wearing jeans and an Iron Maiden t-shirt.

The chief's face looked grim. He'd moved into work mode, and there was no sign of any of the rapport we'd developed, through a lot of ups and downs.

"Gracie, let's go inside and talk. I have questions for you. Especially since Barb was found this close to your bakery."

We walked up the steps and went into the back room, now smelling overwhelmingly like cookies and lime scones.

"Please sit down. Can I get you both coffee?" The two pulled stools up to the metal table.

"Sure, Gracie. I'll take a latte," Brad said with an enthusiastic smile.

"Nothing for me," the chief said with a grunt, directing a judgy look at his deputy. "This is serious. Gracie, it's important that we get your account of what happened—and anything you know about Barb D'Amato's movements today."

I went up to the front counter to make an espresso for Brad, grateful for a moment to breathe before I went back to talk to the chief. He was right—this was serious. My recent hire was dead, about an hour after I'd fired her via phone message for snooping in my office. Not the best way to let someone go, I admit.

Guilt weighed heavy on me. I couldn't blame myself for her death, but I couldn't shake the feeling that her death had something to do with me. That she knew something. Something that had led to her death.

When I came back, the chief had his tablet out, ready to fire away with questions.

I handed Brad his latte and took my seat on a stool across from River Grove's finest. All two of them.

"You hired Barb D'Amato to work at the bakery?" The chief asked sternly. "Is that correct?"

"I hired her and two other applicants. Barb impressed me from the start. She was friendly and had a great sense of humor. Since she'd run her own business for so long, she seemed to understand the importance of customer service. My staff and I interviewed her, and we unanimously decided to hire her." I cleared my throat and looked down at my hands. "Then, today I fired her."

Brad's head popped up, and he set down his latte. "You *fired* her?"

I told them how Rose had called and told me Barb had shown up at the bakery, was wandering around, and had rooted through my office. And after being told not to do it, she did the same thing the next day after sneaking in through the front—while treating a member of the bakery staff disrespectfully.

Brad looked up at me, frowning. He turned to the chief.

As I talked, the chief's expression changed. He paused

for a moment. Brad appeared to be taking notes on his phone. Brad rarely took notes.

"I called her and told her not to bother coming in. We were withdrawing our offer, but we would pay her for her training hours, even ones she hadn't worked yet. I left her a message."

The chief leaned forward, trying to get comfortable on the stool.

"What time did she 'sneak' into the bakery?" The chief asked, using air quotes as he talked.

"This must have been right before Rose called me." I picked up my phone and scrolled through the list of incoming and outgoing calls. "Rose called at 11:08 a.m. Then I called Barb and left the message firing her at 12:25 p.m."

The chief typed up notes.

"You didn't hear back from Barb?" Brad asked.

I shook my head.

"And you didn't see her at the bakery or in the alley till you found her body?" Brad asked, watching my face.

"Nope." Though obviously Barb was very close by, within fifty feet of the bakery's back door, before she was killed. "I was working in the back room and didn't go outside till I left to take coffee and treats to the popup."

I sat for a moment watching them take notes and give each other significant glances.

"Okay, can I ask you a question?" After my short experience with Barb, I needed to get something clear.

The chief shrugged. He shot a significant look at his deputy. "Go ahead, Gracie."

"Barb lived here in town her whole life. Did either of you know her?"

The chief set his tablet down and tried again to adjust

himself to get more comfortable on the stool. He was losing the fight.

"I did. Her shop was in Boulder Creek. Only seven miles away from River Grove, but it looked like she spent most of her time there until it closed. I went up to her house a few years ago when she filed a noise complaint against a neighbor."

"Did she have a problem with following rules?"

The chief tilted his head. "I'll have to check back with the mayor. Corinne knew her better than I did. She said she had a hard time after she had to close Mangia Mama. Corinne just told me Barb seemed different in the past few months. She was worried about her."

"The nosing around that I told you about--did that seem in character for her?"

The chief shrugged. "All I heard from other people in town was, she was up to her neck in debt. Probably why she was willing to take an entry level job at a place like this."

I flinched at his comment but brushed it off. The chief could be blunt. I knew what he meant. It was odd that a fifty-something woman who'd owned her own business would take an entry level job working alongside twenty-somethings.

I nodded. I was trying to come to terms with the puzzle of Barb D'Amato, for the short time I'd known her.

The chief slid off the stool and stood up with a groan. He stretched his arms out and rubbed his lower back. "Too bad you can't have real chairs in here."

He picked up his tablet. "I'm sure we'll have more questions for you and your staff. We'll keep in touch."

Brad stood up and looked around the room curiously, almost as if he were sniffing the air.

"You wouldn't happen to have any of those special chocolate chip cookies you make, would you?"

I went over to the baking trays and picked up two cookies with tongs and tucked them into a small bag for him.

"Thanks, Gracie." Brad's eyes widened as he received the treat. "You got any milk?"

The chief glared at his deputy. For one, his doctor had put him on a no-sweets diet, and he was probably jealous that he couldn't have a cookie. Second, when the police interview a witness, they aren't supposed to come away with goodies.

I had no problem passing them out to our law enforcement team. I grabbed a takeout cup and poured Brad milk from the fridge then fitted a lid down on it.

As I watched them go out the back door, I remembered the glances they'd exchanged during my interview.

I wondered if both of them knew more about Barb D'Amato than they were telling me.

Chapter Eleven

I locked the back door then went up to the front area to sit in the beauty of my newly renovated establishment.

It was my comfort now.

I started the espresso machine and made myself a café americano with a splash of cream. Then I took a seat near the window. River Grovians walked by, some pausing to peer in the windows. When a group knocked on the door, I walked over and pointed at the closed sign with the picture of the yawning loaf and then the hand-drawn one next to it that Beck made—GRAND REOPENING ON MONDAY!

Soon the bright sun coming through the window cast a familiar tall shadow on my table. Nate stood outside, newly tanned and wearing a sweatshirt and shorts.

I opened the door and let him in, tackling him with a hug.

He didn't say anything, just stood and held me for a while. We swayed slightly, my head against his chest. He smelled like trees and fresh air.

"If you want to, tell me the details." He said softly, then inhaled deeply. "This isn't on topic, I know, but you smell amazing."

"It's today's scones." I looked up at him. "I found Barb, one of our new hires, dead in the alley. Want a latte?"

He nodded.

He stood with me while I made it.

I told him everything. For some reason, it calmed me to be doing something else, something normal. I was tempted to not bring it up yet, but he needed to know about the SABRE threat. About Barb's snooping around my office. And why I was worried they were related.

I added the steamed milk to his latte and handed it to him.

"Have you told the agents about Barb?" We sat down at a table.

I shook my head. "I will tonight. Her death may not have anything to do with this."

"Still, do it." He took a big gulp of his latte. "Like you always say, the more info they have, the better."

I can't tell you how good it felt to be able to share these things with Nate—after having to keep my witness protection status from him for the first year of our relationship. I could be myself with him. I didn't have to hide anything. A barrier between us had been removed.

"I feel guilty about Barb being dead," I said, feeling tears sting my eyes. I didn't want to lose it. There was too much to do right now. "She was funny and friendly. Everybody on the staff loved her, and it's going to be hard to tell them. She could be dead because of me."

"You don't know that yet," he said in his reassuring, deep voice, as he held my cold hand in his warm one.

Nate looked around the room. "The last time I saw this

place, it was full of sawdust and plywood. Wanna give me a tour?"

I smiled weakly. "I'd love to."

I took him around the front area, to see the dining area's new flooring and furniture, showing him where we would hang photos. Then I took him behind the counter to our lunch service area and the new order display screens.

He ran his hand along the smooth, curving counter.

"This is stunning, Gracie. It's stylish and modern, but it's also very River Grove."

I leaned against him. "That's what I wanted. It turned out even better than I thought it would. Mostly, I am glad it's *done*."

"I'll have to come get my coffee in person on Monday."

"You'll stand in line then. It's going to be crowded."

His lips turned up slightly, then he spoke in a throaty voice that made my knees weak.

"Oh, yeah? Well, like you, it'll be worth it."

While Nate was leaving out the front door to head home, I heard Rose and Beck in the back room.

I wiped my eyes with a napkin, then went to the back room, where the two were lugging the contents of the cart inside. The trays were empty. They'd sold out, and they'd probably ended up hanging out for a while without much to do but talk till closing time.

"Thanks for handling the popup. I couldn't explain everything on the phone."

Beck looked worried. Rose looked cautious, her eyes wary.

I told them the news about Barb. Beck, who cried when her husband squashed a spider in the bathroom, started sobbing immediately, which I'd expected. Rose just shook her head soberly.

"I can't believe she was shot," Beck said, blotting her face with a tissue. "Poor Barb. How could this happen?"

I hugged her. "I'm not sure, Beck. The chief and Brad are investigating."

Rose frowned, lost in thought. "Do you think she could have—well, maybe rubbed someone the wrong way? Maybe she said or did something that offended someone. Barb could be a lot of fun, but she pretty much said and did whatever she felt like."

I raised my eyebrows. "Unfortunately, there are a lot of people out there like that. They seem to be surviving just fine."

After some prep for tomorrow's lunch training, I asked the two of them to meet in the dining area.

"What's just happened is horrible, but the fact is, we're still reopening Monday. We need to replace Barb. I've got the two other final candidates here—Evan and Daisy. I think we'd be fine offering the position to either one of them —maybe both if we can work it out. I pinged them both by text, and as of this afternoon, they're still available."

"Either one," Beck said, a hitch in her voice as her sobs subsided. "They'd work fine."

"I feel the same way, Gracie." Rose nodded. "They were friendly, and both had food service experience."

While Rose and Gracie cleaned the back room, I called the two candidates. Within a half hour they texted back saying they could come in Sunday for the training.

After Rose left, I called over to Beck, who was wrapping a tub of beignet dough for an overnight rise in the fridge.

"Still up for coming in early tomorrow to hang photos and pictures? Martin from the Frame Hut did everything for us and they look great. I'm getting a couple shots from Nate tonight. I need your artistic expertise, Beck."

Her eyes were still red from crying, but I saw light in her eyes. "That would make me happy."

I hugged her again. "I thought it would."

Chapter Twelve

After Beck left, I called Maeve. She'd be finishing her shift at Pain Parisienne in Napa.

I knew this was going to be a tough conversation.

Maeve broke down after I told her and, once she'd recovered, asked lots of questions I couldn't answer.

"Was it a domestic situation?" She asked, her voice raspy from crying. "These things often are. She said her husband Rocco had passed. But maybe a jealous boyfriend? An angry son-in-law?"

"I don't know much about her family. I hope the chief and Brad are going to look into those possibilities."

Maeve sniffed. "The poor lady had so much hardship in her life. Losing her business, and now this."

I thought for a moment. "Did she talk to you much about her business?"

"Not much. She was angry about it. You remember what she said during training—'Goes to show you can get screwed in a moment's notice. When nobody's going to help you, you gotta take matters into your own hands.'"

"Really? That's what she said?"

"Something like that."

I hung up after talking about reopening plans with Maeve and bringing Evan and Daisy onto the lunch crew. She perked up a little after that.

I needed to get home. I wanted to call the agents, whom I suspected already knew about Barb's death. They always seemed to be up to date on River Grove crime.

I texted my dad and told him what had happened.

I badly wanted to see Nate again. And my little dog.

I didn't get home until 5:45. I sent Nate a text asking if he could lend us a couple of framed prints and if he'd like to come over for dinner at 6:30. My dad was cooking.

He sent a line of laugh emojis.

I can't miss that. I'll bring some framed shots.

Once I got home, I stretched out on the sofa and let Biga settle in the crook of my arm. He slathered my face with slobbery kisses and licked flour off my shirt.

My dad was in the kitchen putting the finishing touches on spaghetti. Mary Jo had taught him how to finish cooking the pasta in the pan of sauce and meat. The difference in flavor was amazing. This had become one of my dad's best dishes.

"You rest, dear," he said, coming out of the kitchen in his apron. "I was sorry to hear the news. Mary Jo called me before you got home and told me. She played some game called Bunker with Barb for years."

I let out a snort. "You mean bunco, right?"

"I suppose. Though I do like the idea of the ladies

hunkered down in trenches rolling dice." He continued chuckling as he went back into the steamy kitchen, and it made me smile to hear him.

I called back to him. "Dad, did you talk to Maura and Jeremy?"

"No, though it sounds like they were calling your burner phone."

I was beat. I didn't want to get up off the sofa. "Can you go get it for me, dad? I put it in a ziplock bag in Biga's food bin."

In one of my recent paranoid moments. Maybe the news about the dissidents had scared me just a little.

"Oh, Gracie." He laughed as he rooted around and I heard dry dog food skitter across the floor. He brought the phone in, smelling vaguely of dog food, and handed it to me.

"Thanks." I hit the contact number. Within a few seconds, Jeremy answered.

"Gracie, we've been trying to get hold of you. We know about Barb D'Amato."

"How did you hear?"

"Our local operative called it in. They thought it might be important."

"I should have filled you in but today was crazy. Barb was a new hire at The Laughing Loaf. One of my employees caught her snooping around my desk. Twice. She hadn't even started work yet. She sneaked in when I wasn't there, and according to my employee, Rose, she headed right for my office."

Jeremy was quiet for a moment. "That is concerning. We'll look into this and see if her name comes up anywhere."

"Any news about the dissidents?" I rubbed my forehead.

Biga licked my face again. With everything going on, my brain hurt.

"No more reports from our sources about your location. But they say the plan to shut down the pipeline is still in play."

I groaned. "Well, that sucks." Secretly, I was glad there wasn't a plan to take out any pipelines here on the west coast.

After hanging up, I showered and dressed in a soft, comfy t-shirt and leggings. Biga must have heard Nate coming up to the door, since he stood there waiting expectantly, his tail wagging.

I looked through the peephole and made sure it was Nate, then opened the door. My dog beat me to him. Nate set his big leather portfolio down against the wall and scooped Biga up. Biga was beside himself with happiness.

My father came into the room, his glasses fogged with steam.

"By my estimates, dinner will be ready in about five minutes."

"Hi, John. Gracie tells me you've perfected your spaghetti skills. I'm looking forward to this."

"No promises, son." My dad held his hands up and looked embarrassed by the compliment. "But I do think you'll like it."

When my dad retreated to the kitchen, Nate brought over his portfolio.

"I'd love to see what you've got," I said, patting the seat next to me on the sofa.

"I went for small-*ish*, based on the wall space you have." He opened the flap and took out a framed, matted color photo of a hawk spreading his wings in a bright blue sky, about 12 x 18 inches. Then a stark black and white photo of a finch, taken on his trip to the Galapagos Islands last year, matted in an 18 x 18-inch square frame. He'd signed *Nathaniel Behrens* on the matte on each. His signature looked like a work of art itself, with creative loops and a crossed *t* that resembled a swooping bird.

In the square-framed print, the finch stood on a rock overlooking the ocean. The precise detail on the little bird was incredible, and his dark form contrasted against the sunny, white rock. It was hard to look away from the photo —its composition and contrast were just so interesting.

"I feel like he's staring into my soul," I said.

Nate smiled and kissed my hand. "He is. The wise finch knows *all*."

"Thank you for these," I moved closer to him on the sofa. "Beck and I are hanging everything tomorrow. Do you want these to be for sale?"

Nate shook his head. "No, not needed. I'm happy for these to be on display at The Laughing Loaf. The only photos I sell are the ones I do on commission."

"I love them." I leaned against him. "We will take good care of them. Thank you."

My dad called us to the table, where we dished ourselves up spaghetti and salad. I poured glasses of Zinfandel for the three of us. The rich, slightly sweet red wine tasted great with the marinara.

Biga watched us from his food bowl, sulking that he wasn't invited.

"The agents know Barb was shot." I sat back, after scarfing down most of the spaghetti on my plate. "Their local contact called them right away."

"Wait—I heard you mention this contact before," Nate said, pausing to take a sip of wine. "Who is this person?"

"The agents won't tell us," my dad said with a shrug.

"Gracie and I have had a lot of fun speculating about it. We've suspected the chief, Mayor C, even Reggie McFerrin."

"We've decided it couldn't be the chief, though he *does* know we're in WITSEC." I picked up a cherry tomato that had strayed from my salad and popped it in my mouth. "And I asked the chief—he said it's not Mayor C."

"Not sure about Reggie." My father swirled his wine glass. "I can't imagine him working for the government."

Nate watched us over his wine glass, amused. "Wouldn't he be the best person for the job? Who would suspect a former hippie who runs a music venue?"

My dad nodded. "Point taken, Nate."

"Gracie, you said you met with the chief and Brad Castro right after you found Barb's body. They were probably the first to find out. What if the contact is Brad? He could have called the agents from the crime scene in the alley."

I'd considered this possibility, but never seriously. I'd always written Brad off as young and inexperienced, barely out of high school, and a little bit of a goofball. Then I remembered the back-and-forth glances Brad and the chief gave each other while they'd interviewed me at the bakery. Maybe Brad knew more than I thought about my WITSEC status.

"Maybe he doesn't really work part-time at Best Buy," my dad said, supporting his chin with his hand, in thinking mode.

"Those heavy metal t-shirts are just a clever disguise," Nate said with a grin.

"Maybe it's my imagination, but when I met with the chief and Brad today, they kept exchanging glances. Like they knew something I didn't." It was amusing to think of, but Brad could be the perfect River Grove contact. As deputy, he had an excuse to be anywhere around town. He could be keeping an eye on my dad and me, and no one would ever suspect.

I thought about him in the bakery's back room, asking for chocolate chip cookies and a glass of milk.

We'd finished our wine at this point. I went into the kitchen to make Nate and me espresso shots using the little moka pot he'd brought for post-dinner coffee. The three of us had gotten a little loopy with our suggestions. It had been a long, hard day.

Still, I wondered if there was something to our theory.

Chapter Thirteen

While I finished post-meal cleanup, Nate played a game of chess with my dad.

Big surprise, he lost.

After showing my dad and me highlights of his trip, including some breathtaking waterfall photos, the two of us spent some time cuddling in the front porch swing.

I convinced him to take a quick trip with me to the bakery to set up Biga's new bed and toys for his return to the bakery tomorrow.

We laughed and tried out the interactive toys in his pen. After today's tragedy, it felt good to have a positive time at the bakery.

Nate dropped me off at home, with an epic kissing session at the door. Then he left to get a good night's sleep after a long drive and busy week of shooting.

I came inside, feeling better after a hard day, though a little woozy from the snogging.

When I picked up my phone, I saw a long string of new texts.

All of them were from my best friend, Elana. She hated not being in the loop.

> GIRL! I heard what happened today.

> What the hell? One of your employees was MURDERED?!

> CALL ME!

> Gracie – are you even there? Tell me what's going on

> Are you ok?

> I need to know what happened.

> NOW!!!

WITH BIGA RIGHT BEHIND ME, I headed for my room, closed the door, and flopped down onto my bed. Biga jumped up and settled in next to me.

I hit Elana's contact on my cell phone and gave her a call.

"Gracie, what is going on?" The energy in my friend's voice made me feel exhausted in comparison. I'd been up since 4 a.m. and it was now 9:40 p.m.

I told her about finding Barb in the alley, then gave her a summary of what Barb had been like and about her snooping in my office.

"Her behavior was suspicious. It seemed like she was after info on me personally."

Elana made sympathetic noises then finally said,

bluntly. "You're worried that she might find out about you being, uh, in witness protection."

I couldn't share with Elana about the SABRE threat—or anything else I heard from the agents. Elana gabbed and almost couldn't help herself. I was careful not to tell her anything that would be dangerous to let slip.

"I guess it was something like that," I said vaguely, rubbing Biga's belly.

"She was shot. In the heart?" Elana paused to think about this then continued with great seriousness. "That's big-city crime. Like some kind of mafia stuff."

"As far as I know, the mafia doesn't have a *big* presence in the Santa Cruz Mountains." I stifled a laugh, "But it could have been some other kind of organization. The chief did say that the shot was very targeted. She died almost instantly. This doesn't seem like the work of an amateur."

"But why *Barb*..." The way Elana's voice trailed off, I knew she was going into crime-solving mode.

"Did you ever meet her?" I asked. Elana knew most people in town. She regularly engaged in gossip and could usually give me a complete dossier on anyone I was curious about.

"I chatted with her at a cookoff one year. The woman liked to talk. And she was funny, so it was an entertaining conversation." Elana paused. "Oh, and I checked out her food imports shop in Boulder Creek. Mangia something. What a fun store. They gave out samples. I bought some mortadella and really good 24-month aged Parmigiano-Reggiano there."

These details didn't exactly shed light on Barb's life or her murder. But what I was hearing about Barb was, she was a tough, hardworking woman who was heartbroken that she had to close her shop.

She had no dark secrets in her life, at least that I could see. Nothing that seemed to point to her having connections with the underworld or even with Satrovanian dissidents.

"I need to talk to Mayor C." Biga had fallen asleep on my arm. I needed my arm back since I was starting to lose feeling in it. I gently pulled it out from under him. Biga woke, startled. "The chief said Corinne knew her. She noticed Barb really changed after she lost her shop." I remembered something Barb said at the Laughing Loaf orientation.

"Barb said she was mad about having to shut down her shop, but her husband Rocco used to say—"

"Her husband's name is Rocco?" Elana snorted. "That sounds like a mafia name to me."

I rolled my eyes at Elana's comment and continued.

"*Rocco* used to say something about Barb always finding a way out of a problem and landing on her feet. Maybe she found a way to get her business back—but had to get help from some dangerous people."

"Maybe *loan* sharks," Elana said ominously.

"Oh, sure. Because there are so *many* of them around here," I said with a big dollop of snark.

"Gracie, don't laugh. It might explain why she was shot. She couldn't pay the money back."

It was always fun to talk crime-solving with Elana. Sometimes bouncing ideas of each other resulted in a break-through and a new way to view the situation. But I wasn't ready to track down a killer. Tomorrow Beck and I would put the final touches on the bakery and train our new lunch crew members.

Then Monday was show time—the big reveal after three months of planning and hard work. The bakery would be busy all week, as customers from River Grove and beyond came in to see the debut of our renovated space.

We'd be working the bugs out of our lunch service and, realistically, learning how to operate in a new space—with four new employees and Rose, who hadn't served customers in the bakery itself yet.

Did I have time to solve Barb's murder? Absolutely not.

Chapter Fourteen

The next morning, I woke at 4 a.m. out of habit. I wasn't meeting Beck till 7:30. I was bubbling over with anticipation that almost took my mind off yesterday's troubling events.

The renovated bakery looked beautiful, and I couldn't wait to reveal it to customers. Today was for finishing touches on our new space. The frosting on the cinnamon rolls. The Dutch crunch on top of the bread loaf. The decorative leaf patterns cut into our whole wheat sourdough loaves with my scorer.

You get the idea.

I'd set out my clothes the night before and had Biga's crate ready to lure him into. I was excited to show him his "renovated" pen at The Laughing Loaf. I was glad Nate and I were able to sneak over and set it up. He had been almost as excited as I was about Biga getting something special in his area of the bakery.

I had plenty of time, so I loaded the framed art into the back of my car, then went inside to make a legit cup of coffee on the stove with the moka pot Nate had left at our house last night. I warmed up last night's spaghetti leftovers in the microwave. They tasted even better the next day. I devoured them with my strong cup of espresso and searched for news on my phone.

I wanted to see how local news was covering Barb's death.

The headlines didn't make our little town look good.

ANOTHER MURDER STRIKES TINY TOWN

Shopkeeper Victim of River Grove Shooting

Longtime Boulder Creek Merchant D'Amato
Dies in Shooting

River Grove Shooting
Takes Life of Mangia Mama's D'Amato

The chief and Mayor C, earnest defenders of River Grove's public safety record, would not be happy.

Scanning the articles, I gathered that most people knew Barb from her shop. The article quoted the shop's former assistant manager Carlene McAffrey: "Barb's enthusiasm and big heart brought customers in. And now this happened. It seems so heartbreaking. So unfair."

Another article showed a photo of a younger, slimmer Barb with her smiling daughter, Rosanna, and husband, Rocco. They stood at the top of the hill, holding their mats in front of them, ready to slide down the muddy hill on River Grove's Flume Run Day about ten years ago. The Flume Run was another one of my town's quaint traditions. It commemorated River Grove's logging past in the 1880s, when loggers pushed redwood logs down the wet hills to the train station for transport to ships on the coast.

According to the article, Rocco died of lung cancer five years ago. Rosanna was now married and lived up the coast in Half Moon Bay.

I was starting to see Barb as someone who'd had a series of bad things happen to her, things that most likely were not her fault. Maeve had been right about Barb. She was energetic, resilient, and funny. Her rapport with customers would have been an asset to The Laughing Loaf.

I took Biga out in the backyard and played with him for a while to get my mind off the loss of Barb. I'd be busy this week, so why not enjoy as much play time with him as possible?

A little past 7 a.m., in the cool morning light, Biga and I took off for The Laughing Loaf.

Beck's car was already parked in the alley. Maybe she'd been unable to sleep in, too. I shouldered my bag and took Biga in my arms. We headed up the back steps.

Beck was at one of the tables, piping whipped cream onto what looked like a tray of tarts.

"Good morning!" I called, and she turned to me, startled.

"Whaaaa-aa! I was hoping to surprise you." She gave me a sheepish look and backed against the table to hide what she was working on.

I had my suspicions as to what she was doing.

I raised an eyebrow and smirked.

"I'm taking Biga to see the new stuff in his pen. When he's settled, I'd love to come see what you're working on."

I took Biga into his room off the back room and reached over the gate to let him down. He stood still eyeing the new toys and bed suspiciously. I bent over the fence and turned on one of the interactive toys, a ball which started lurching in circles. As it eased in his direction, Biga jumped back and barked at the toy. Then he trotted over to his new bed and curled up in it, his eyes locked on the mechanical intruder.

I reached over the fence, grabbed the toy, and turned it off.

"I'm sorry, Biga. A little too much for you today. I get it." I took out one of his liver treats and held it up. He got off his bed and rushed over to me, standing on his hind legs to get it from my hand.

"Good job, Biga Boy." I ruffled the fur on his head. "Welcome back to your pen. I'll take you out for a walk later, I promise."

When I went to the back room, I saw the tray of beautiful whipped-cream-topped treats.

"I'm all done! Would you like one?" Beck plated one of the tarts and handed it to me with a fork.

"This is the strawberry shortbread tart," she said, pride in her eyes. "I finally got a version I feel good about."

"I *thought* that was what you were working on," I said as I received the plate. "This will be a nice dessert after my leftover spaghetti breakfast. I've been excited to try this."

I sunk the edge of the fork into the tart, feeling it sink down from the whipped cream into flaky tart crust.

I closed my eyes and ate the bite. I hate that word "mouthfeel," but this was a feast for my mouth and all my senses. First the creamy topping, then the smell and taste of fresh, just-ripe strawberries, then the rich crème anglaise and buttery crust. It was a beautiful combination of flavors and textures.

"This is so good." I swallowed and took another bite.

"The perfect summer dessert. Or breakfast. Let's put this on our opening week menu as a special."

Beck's face lit up. "I'm so glad. I had a lot of different versions, but I liked the layers in this one. I learned to make crème anglaise in my pastry class in San Francisco. I want to put it on *everything* now."

Last year, I'd established an education fund for Beck, so she could take baking classes and enhance her already impressive pastry skills.

"Not that I blame you," I said, laughing. "That creaminess is great next to the tart crust. How about let's save the rest for the trainees."

"Great idea!" Beck smiled, covering the tray so she could keep the tarts chilled in the fridge till then.

Since my bread baker Maeve wasn't here on weekends, I took out some discard and fed the sourdough starter more flour and water in its vat, using a paddle to stir the gloppy mixture. I'd save the discard for more chocolate chip sourdough cookies.

When Beck had washed her hands and was ready, we carried in the boxes of framed photos for hanging in the front area. We'd hang the historical reproductions from River Grove history on the long tan wall behind the tables. As I looked through them, that fondness for my little town welled up in me so strongly that I almost cried. I felt grafted into this tiny town—like a branch a gardener had attached to a very different species of tree, then tended till it thrived.

"Do you think we need to hang them in order of their time period?" Beck asked as she surveyed the framed reproductions.

"I don't think we have to. It's not like this is a museum exhibit. Let's try things out and decide what looks interesting."

Beck nodded. "Let's do it."

We laid the photos out across the new, shiny hardwood floor, then stood back and looked at them. We both walked back and forth, surveying the bunch.

"This one of the log flumes really catches your eye." Beck picked up the sepia-toned photo of workers at the top of the hill, pushing logs down the flume. "I want to put this one where people see it right away."

"Let's put it above the straws, sleeves and napkin cart, over here." I pointed to the back wall of the dining area.

Artistic Beck had the skills for hanging art. She opened the hanging kit and took out a hanger and a nail. I watched as she set up the hanger. I handed her the photo, and she adjusted it on its wire till it hung straight.

"Oh, yeah. I love it there." I stepped back to view it in place. The sepia tone of the photo complemented the golden-brown wooden cart perfectly. "One down, eleven to go."

Over the next hour and a half, we hung all the photos. We switched a few around until we felt satisfied.

We ended up hanging Nate's bird photos near the entrance. They'd be one of the first things customers saw coming in. They were different enough from the historical photos and it made sense.

We walked around the front area, admiring everything and relishing the look of our new bakery. Then we put on an old favorite pop song on the sound system and did a happy dance on the new floor, singing along to the song at the top of our lungs. I'm sure any passersby at that hour thought we'd completely lost it.

"Wait!" I clicked on my phone to stop the music playing through the bakery's speakers. "I forgot one important thing." I ran back to my office and brought out a box of things from the front that we'd taken down before renovation. I wanted to make sure I put them up.

I rooted through the box.

Beck's painting was not here.

I turned the box out onto my desk.

Last year, Beck had painted a small square picture of me holding Biga in front of The Laughing Loaf Bakery. Beck had painted it in her usual, fanciful style, but it looked like me and it looked like Biga. She'd captured everything. The old bank building, the Laughing Loaf sign.

It was one of my favorite possessions. I didn't want to reopen the bakery without it on display.

"You sure it was in the box with the other stuff?" Beck asked. "Maybe you took it home?"

"I wanted to keep it here. That box had everything from the front area that I wanted to save." I said, anger chewing at my insides. I thought of Barb nosing around my desk. Could she have taken it? It didn't make sense. Why that painting?

"I'll look at home. And check my car." I shook my head, trying to think of anywhere else it could be.

Beck and I weren't in a crunch to prep for the next day, and we had some leisure to talk and enjoy ourselves.

I'd started with Beck, when she'd been a shy twenty-two-year-old with no work experience other than the daycare program at her church. It wasn't like I was qualified to be opening a bakery myself. I'd only ever worked in the tech industry. I'd baked a lot, but I had no retail experience in breadmaking and was starting over in a completely new town.

Together we'd turned the former bank and burger joint into a local meeting place for River Grovians, and we'd become a go-to place for baked goods from San Jose to the coast.

AFTER WE FINISHED HANGING the pictures, we made lattes and sat down in the dining area with turkey and avocado sandwiches on sourdough that we'd made for ourselves.

"Are we ready for tomorrow's rush?" I asked, as we watched people put their faces up to the windows to peer in at the renovated space. I wanted to wave, but I also didn't want them to think we'd let them in for an advanced peek.

"I think it's going to be crowded," Beck said, a little apprehensively. "But it's going to be a lot of fun. My whole family is coming in, like *everybody*. All my nieces and nephews."

"I've got some chocolate chip cookie and gingerbread dough mixed up to bake later." I said, smiling. "We'll have something to give the kids. And maybe some adults—at least, the ones we *like*."

Beck giggled. "I can think of a few that don't deserve cookies."

I laughed. Beck was always kind to everybody who came in, whether they deserved it or not.

I thought about what Beck had told me a few days ago.

"By the way, what's the grandkid count so far—boys versus girls?"

Beck counted on her fingers. "Four boys and two girls."

"And what are you and Sam hoping for?"

Beck laughed and I saw her light brown skin tinged with a blush. "Sam wants a girl. I'm good with that. I had enough boys in my life growing up." Beck had five older brothers.

I smiled and downed the last of my latte. "I hope you get your wish."

Everything was ready for when the trainees came in at 1 p.m. Our bread options were sliced and on the counter. We'd set out meats, lettuce, tomatoes, sliced avocados, cheeses, toppings, and spreads. The under-the-counter fridge was filled with milks, and the syrup rack had all our coffee additions. We'd filled the display case with a small sampler of our rolls, muffins, scones, and tarts, so the staff could become familiar with what we offered.

Training went well, and we got to know our latest hires, Daisy and Evan, better. Evan knew both Elise and Tyler. Both of our newest hires had come into the bakery many times, which helped.

I kept the door unlocked but hung a sign on it, under the snoozing Laughing Loaf sign:

Closed today for staff training.

I'd invited Chloe Westerman, the chief, and Mayor C to serve as test customers for our session. Nate was going to stop by, too, if he had time. I told them all to act as they normally would when they came into the bakery. While our trainees took turns, two by two, working the lunch counter, I manned the espresso machine.

Around 1:15, Chloe came in, her hair in a bouncy ponytail, wearing a tie-dyed t-shirt, cutoff shorts, and Birkenstocks. As she came to the door, I saw her smile and blow a kiss to someone just beyond the window. Could it be Jeb?

She perused the sandwich list then made her choice. Tyler took her order.

"I'd like a veggie sandwich, with extra roasted red peppers and avocado, and all the produce you've got, and I mean that seriously. On whole wheat bread. Oh, and a bottle of water."

"Got it." Tyler took the order and rang her up. "Cheese?"

"Not unless it's vegan. And can you toast the bread so it's sort of a medium-brown."

The corners of Tyler's mouth turned up in a grin as he nodded and started to make her sandwich. Chloe looked adorable today, and she was being a little sassy.

"Will that be for here or to go?"

"To go, since I'm meeting a friend in the park."

Chloe received her lunch in a bag at the pickup station. "Thank you!" she called, heading for the door.

Ten minutes later, the chief came in. He'd interviewed me in the back room after Barb's death, but he hadn't seen the renovated front area yet. Now he looked around the place, examining the photos and then slowly making his way over to order. He nodded over to me at the espresso machine.

"I'll take a latte with oat milk, please. Why'nt you make me a ham sandwich with cheddar cheese on sourdough. None of that sandwich spread. If you can put a fried egg on it, that would be great. I'll eat it here. I want to check out the dining area."

Elise, who was entering his sandwich on the order system, looked over at me anxiously.

"Let me see if we can get that for you, chief."

"I'll get Beck to make the egg," I told her. I popped my head through the doorway to the back room to ask Beck, who was having Daisy and Evan fill out their employee paperwork.

"Sure, I can do that," she said cheerfully. "I'll have it in five minutes."

As he waited, the chief came over to the counter by the espresso machine where I was making his latte. He leaned an elbow on the counter.

"The mayor's meeting me here in a few minutes." He looked around the counter area. "We've got to stake out our new meeting spot."

"Sounds like a great idea, chief." I handed him his steaming latte.

"I'm sure looking forward to walking across the street to get my lunch." His eyes crinkled up in a smile. "Nice touch with all those River Grove photos."

Beck came out to deliver the fried egg on a plate, and Tyler and Elise soon had the chief's sandwich waiting for him at pickup. He took his lunch over to the dining area, looked around at his options, and then settled in at a table at the back of the room.

I saw Mayor C's short, stocky form enter the front door, a grim look on her face as usual. She was clutching a notebook full of papers and looked distracted. She went over to study Nate's photos, then came up to the counter.

"Hi, Mayor C," Elise said cheerfully. "What can I get for you today?"

"Hello, Elise." The mayor studied the lunch menu for a moment. "I see you have wraps. I'll take a chicken wrap with avocado, tomatoes, and jalapenos. Can you tell me if the avocado is fresh?"

Elise nodded and smiled. "We sliced it ourselves about an hour ago."

"What is the wrap made of?" The mayor asked with some skepticism. "Is it purchased somewhere else?"

Elise brightened. "It's flatbread that we make here in the bakery. I just had a sample. It's *so* good."

"Okay, fine," The mayor said almost begrudgingly. "Give me the wrap and a small hazelnut latte with oat milk."

Elise entered the order in the system, and I started on the mayor's latte.

"Barb D'Amato would have been here today," the mayor said after heading over to my end of the counter.

I wasn't going to explain to the mayor that I'd fired Barb, so she wouldn't have been here today even if she hadn't been murdered. I added two pumps of hazelnut syrup to her drink and simply nodded.

"I heard you knew her."

The mayor sighed and looked down at her phone. "She was involved in the River Grove Women's Club with me for years. Until she had to close her shop. Then we lost touch. She was struggling. I called her a few times, but she never got back to me." The mayor frowned. "And now she's dead."

Maybe it was last night's conversation with Elana prompting me, but I had to ask. "Do you think she could have been desperate enough to get money from less-than-desirable people?"

The mayor grimaced. "I don't know where she would have made those connections. But she was desperate." Her voice wavered, and I wondered if the mayor was even getting a little emotional about the loss of Barb. "She was shot in broad daylight, and obviously targeted. It's not like I haven't thought about that possibility."

I handed the mayor her latte, and Tyler told her the wrap was ready at pickup.

I saw her smile warmly as she saw the chief sitting at the back table. He gave her a friendly wave. She picked up her meal and went to sit down with him at their new meeting place.

Somehow, all was right with the world when our town's police chief and our mayor were sitting together, happily talking about crime.

I went over a few details with Tyler and Elise, and Tyler mentioned ways to set up the sandwich line that had worked well at his previous employer, so we rearranged a few things. Evan and Daisy worked the counter next, taking their places after donning their Laughing Loaf aprons.

Beck came out with them and ordered a wrap for herself. Daisy, I noticed, was a little nervous. With encouragement from cheery Beck, she seemed to relax. Soon she was inputting the order in the system, tag-teaming with Evan on the food prep, and telling Beck her order was at pickup with a friendly smile.

As I watched these reserved, earnest twenty-somethings do their job, I missed Barb, with her humor and crazy, outgoing nature. She'd given us an energy we just didn't have now.

I hoped Nate would stop by. I wanted him to go through the lunch station—order a wrap because they were delicious—and see his photos hung up. I was thrilled with how the renovation had turned out, and I wanted him to share that with me. Still, he was on a tight deadline with his photos. He'd also gotten up early to hike 15 miles uphill to a waterfall in Yosemite yesterday. If he couldn't make it today, there would be another time for it.

We were almost done with our training and orientation when Nate came through the front door, wearing shorts and sandals, since the warm day called for them. He didn't look like a dork in them either. His muscular legs looked, well, really amazing. I saw him smile at his framed photos.

The mayor and the chief called out from their table as they saw him come in.

"Nate, welcome back!" the mayor called out.

The chief waved. "Wrestle any bears up there, son?"

Nate laughed. "Nah. We mostly played board games."

He stood in front of the menu, then stepped up to the counter, where Evan took his order.

"I'd like a turkey and avocado wrap, all the veggies and no cheese or spread, and extra jalapenos. Are you serving coffee today?" I nodded in response. "Then I'd love an iced latte with nonfat milk."

"Got it," Evan said, entering the order. Daisy looked a little nervous as she spread out the flatbread and began layering on the items.

Nate came over to the counter by the espresso machine as I got ready to prepare his drink. He leaned over the counter and planted a kiss on my cheek. I glanced at my new hires and saw that Daisy had seen us and was looking a bit shocked.

"The photos look great up there, Gracie."

"My assistant manager's choice. She's the one with the artistic eye."

"Looks like things are going well," he said looking around the front area.

"Considering yesterday, they are." I kept my voice low since I hadn't talked to my newest employees about Barb's death. "Things are still—well, a little fresh. We're trying to carry on."

"No word from the chief about the investigation?"

I watched the chief gesture as he talked to the mayor at the back table. "I'll check in with him, but I don't think so."

"I'll have to grab my wrap and get back to my photos,"

Nate said, looking toward the pickup counter where a bag sat waiting. "Talk to you tonight?"

"Of course." I reached up to give him one more peck on the cheek.

I locked the front door, and Beck and I gave some last-minute instructions to our lunch crew for tomorrow.

We sat down together and chatted while enjoying Beck's Strawberry Shortbread Tarts.

"These taste like summer," Elise said, pausing after eating half her tart.

"So we're going to be selling these at the bakery, right?" Tyler asked.

"Of course we are," I smiled over at Beck. "They'll be on the menu very soon."

The lunch crew hung up their aprons and took off to enjoy the rest of a warm Sunday afternoon.

Beck and I got to work on prep for Monday's bakes.

We played one of our really old playlists and sang along.

It felt right that today was just Beck and me, working together as we had in the beginning. We were heading into a season of changes.

This day was the calm before the storm. Tomorrow, I expected the bakery to be flooded with customers, eager to check out our new bakery.

There was something I didn't expect, though.

Tomorrow would thrust me into a whole new level of danger.

Chapter Fifteen

efore we locked up, Beck and I sat down for a catch-up meeting.

"You must be feeling good about the lunch crew." Beck said, as she stifled a yawn. It was 6 p.m. and it felt like we'd worked a very long day.

"They did well." I leaned on my hand as I picked up the delicious crumbs from a strawberry shortbread tart. "Obviously without the pressure we'll have tomorrow, but I think they'll be fine. Daisy seemed nervous, but her first shift will be Tuesday, when it won't be opening day crowds."

"We're all set as far as the back room goes," Beck said, looking at a printout of tomorrow morning's offerings and quantities. "Maeve's handling sandwich breads. Rose is coming in early to help with the beignets. We may have people fighting each other to get those. I've doubled the quantities."

I grinned as I said, "If there are fights, it's your fault for making them so good."

Beck smiled like the Cheshire Cat. "It *might* be my fault."

"The photos all look great. Thanks for your help, Beck."

We hugged and walked out together into a pleasantly warm evening.

I woke the next morning at 3:30 a.m., unable to sleep any longer.

It was Monday. Show time.

I made a quick pre-coffee, loaded it with cream, and gulped it down. I slipped my burner phone into my purse. I don't know why I thought to do it, but I'm glad I did.

Biga was not ready to wake, however, and reluctantly stumbled into his carrier with the speed and grace of a canine zombie.

"Biga boy, it's not your usual time. But this will give you lots of time to play with those interactive toys you love so much."

As I did whenever I came into the bakery in the dark, I immediately locked the back door and turned on every light in the place, then used my phone to connect to the sound system and start up a jumping playlist. It was an early Van Halen morning, not sure why. But it got me going. Might as well jump, right?

I set Biga up in his pen, filled his water and food bowls, then got to work.

Beck came in earlier than usual, too, followed by Maeve and Rose an hour later. The back room smelled of caramel, cinnamon and the sweet, deep-fried goodness of beignets. Rose manned the two frying pots on the stove, carefully turning the pillowy treats until they were a perfect golden brown.

I'd work the counter, and Maeve would be with me during our high times—right after opening and then in that hour before lunch service. Rose was on the espresso machine, and Beck would fill in there when needed.

With a pounding in my chest, I set the Laughing Loaf Joke of the Day on its stand. These were all dad jokes, a reminder of when I was fifteen, after my mother passed. My dad and I needed anything to make us laugh so we went for the dad jokes.

Today's was groan worthy:

The Laughing Loaf Joke of the Day
I ordered a chicken and an egg online.
I'll let you know which comes first.

We were ready. I looked out our big front windows at the line forming. There'd been a few people at 7 a.m. which I thought was encouraging. Devoted customers who wanted to be the first in.

Now it was 7:25. I went into the dining room to look out and see how long this line really was.

It now stretched from our front door down the block to Loudon Lane, then I saw that it went beyond the corner, past the Key Haus.

I don't know why I was feeling emotional, but tears filled my eyes. I couldn't believe so many people wanted to come see us reopen.

"Hey, everybody!" I poked my head through the doorway to the back room. "If you can, come see this."

Beck, Maeve, and Rose ran into the front area and looked out.

"Oh, my God," Rose called out. "That's just crazy!"

"Let me take a picture," Maeve pulled her phone out of her apron. "We need to put this out on social media." She went to the window so she could capture as much of the line as possible. She snapped a few shots.

Beck smiled and I felt better, since she had started to blot her eyes with a tissue. "This is amazing. This looks like half of the town. Okay, maybe not but it's a *lot*."

"According to my phone, it's 7:29:30." Maeve said. "In 20 seconds, let's do a countdown."

On Maeve's cue, we all started. "10-9-8-7-6-5-4-3-2-and ONE!" We yelled together at the top of our lungs.

"Should I release the hounds?" Maeve headed to the front door, grinning mischievously.

"Do it," I said, running back to the counter. "Stop the line at the door when there's ten inside."

Maeve opened the door, instructing people to form a line inside then serving as bouncer, to make sure we didn't get an onrush of customers going past our capacity limits.

I smiled, took orders on the new system, and filled plates and bags with pastries, while Rose worked on coffee orders. I saw River Grovians, friends and acquaintances from around town. I even recognized some customers who'd come in from Santa Cruz for the occasion. We replaced trays in the display case three times before lunch service started.

Adrenaline kept us moving fast, until the line was down to six people inside—at about 8:15 a.m.

At one point, Rose moved over to the counter to take orders while I crouched down behind the counter and grabbed a streusel muffin from the display case. I was tired already and really hungry.

The dining area was full, and the noise level at the bakery was high, as customers ate their pastries and sipped their coffee drinks, chattering away with each other. New customers stopped by and joined conversations with friends.

We didn't have as many students as we would have had during the school year, but I did see Dakota Li, Amelia Gruber, and Chloe, along with a few other high schoolers, who'd pushed their chairs together at a very small table to chat.

After finishing my muffin surreptitiously, I looked up to see Kirk and Elana Schiffer at the counter. It had been killing Elana to not have a sneak peek at the renovation. She'd wanted to see it so badly, but I'd only allowed a few people to see it before opening day.

"Gracie, the place is absolutely gorgeous." She looked around her and then gave me a raised eyebrow. "What a reveal today. I *guess* I forgive you for keeping it secret."

Kirk laughed and put his arm around his wife. "It was worth the wait. We're both on our way to work but we had to be here for the opening to support you. Can we have lattes with 2 percent milk and a couple of cinnamon rolls?"

Later, Beck's three oldest brothers—Matthew, Zachary, and Joshua—came in with their combined brood of six kids under the age of seven. Beck came out from the back, squealed with glee, and hugged everybody. She must have had favored auntie status, because the younger kids began climbing on her and smothering her with hugs—even before they got any cookies.

The two of us handed out cookies and then juice boxes, probably guaranteeing them all sugar highs for the rest of the day.

By the time the lunch counter opened at 11 a.m., I was beat. I wanted to curl up in Biga's bed and take a nap.

Thankfully the morning's big rush ended, and the number of customers coming in for lunch was large but reasonable. We did run out of sliced turkey and bottled water but had no serious problems--other than not having enough room in the dining area for everyone who wanted to eat at the bakery.

The chief and Mayor C came over for lunch, along with Jake and Jeanne Daniels, Brad Castro, Hank and Victor Schulz from the Key Haus, and even Mary Jo and my dad, who were going to take their lunch to-go for a picnic on the greenspace. Marla from Spinnetti's Sparkletown Cleaners eased in the door shyly and took her place in line. I nodded at her, and she smiled.

Customers complimented us on the renovated space and cycled through looking at the old photos of River Grove. At least one customer asked if he could buy Nate's photos.

At 12:30, I left Beck in charge at the counter and took Biga for a walk. Biga and I both needed it. Biga pulled on the leash, happy to be free from his pen. We took our usual route, crossing the alley to the trail that followed the San Luciano River. I stood for a moment as we hit the trail, taking in the silence that enveloped us after the noise of the crowded bakery.

The day was heating up, and the cool shade under the tree-sheltered path felt refreshing. Biga started to slow down, stopping at every one of his favorite bushes along the path. He must have been going crazy in his pen, away from the action. He looked up at me, his tail wagging.

We're really doing this? We get to go outside?

I knew for a fact that, for the past two months, my father's default plan for letting Biga get exercise was standing at our back door, throwing his toys into the yard and letting Biga bring them back to him.

Away from the noise, as we walked down the trail, I

started to think about Barb and what had just happened two days ago.

Barb had been hard up for cash. Her life's dream had just fallen apart, and she needed cash to put it back together. She was desperate enough for money to live on that she'd applied to work on the lunch crew. But how had she planned on getting enough money to bring her business back?

Mayor C had also wondered if Barb had looked for dangerous ways to get cash. Desperation tends to lower your standards as far as what help you're willing to ask for and receive.

Maybe she'd taken on a loan, sure that she could pay it back in time. Her Mangia Mama shop had been profitable, so maybe she'd been overconfident she'd be able to pay it back if she got the shop back.

I thought about who in town might have known Barb well. Mayor C did, through the women's club. Jeanne Daniels would be about Barb's age. Barb was extroverted, and I'd be willing to bet she'd been close to people in River Grove, people she might have confided in. I just needed to find out who these people were.

As we passed the back of The Riverside Saloon, I noticed they'd opened the back deck for customers. A few patrons sat nursing their drinks, looking out at a beautiful view of the San Luciano River, shimmering in the sun.

Reggie stood at the railing, sun reflecting off his mirrored aviator sunglasses. When he saw me, he waved. I waved back and after Biga saw his favorite person, his tail began wagging like crazy.

Within a minute or two, Reggie came down the side stairs and met me on the trail. Biga was beside himself. He put his paws up on Reggie's legs. Reggie scooped him up and held him close.

"You've made his day," I said with a laugh. "He wasn't happy to be in his pen with the bakery full of customers—and all that food around."

"Poor guy." Reggie smiled and scratched Biga's belly. "A few of my staff stopped by The Laughing Loaf on their way to work. They said it was packed."

"The line went down the street for almost two blocks. It was overwhelming. It scares me." I looked down at my feet for some reason. I didn't know why. I didn't want to look at Reggie. I knew he was going to say something deep that would make me think. I didn't want to think.

It made me happy that everyone wanted to see the new bakery, but I was still afraid that the bakery's notoriety would expose my identity. To Russian spies. To Satrovanian dissidents. I mean, it had happened once. It could happen again.

"Gracie, I think you want to keep your bakery small," Reggie said, invisible behind his shades. "To keep your life simple. Avoid pain, avoid mistakes from your past. It's not your choice."

"What?" I looked up suddenly. "What do you mean?"

"The bakery is something you set in motion, just like I opened The Riverside years ago. It's not my thing anymore. The staff, the chefs, the musicians, they all work together to make something special. The bakery isn't just you—it's a community. It's not dependent on you. Release it to the world, Gracie."

He set Biga down, and my little dog headed toward a bush and gave it a good watering. Reggie looked thoughtful for a moment. "I think you're learning to do that."

Reggie's mind was on a completely different plane than

mine most of the time. Still, there was something to what he was saying. I did need to let go. I could not control everything.

But I don't think Reggie understood exactly *why* I was afraid. The bigger the bakery got and the more my name was associated with it, the easier it would be for dissidents, spies, or foreign governments to track me down.

Reggie didn't understand what I was really worried about. So I didn't think he was the local operative.

He would have known the dissidents were trying to find me. Judging by his words, he didn't.

Still, Reggie made sense. The Laughing Loaf wasn't just mine. It belonged to Beck, Maeve, Rose, the lunch crew, and all the people who'd lined up this morning for the reopening.

Two years ago, I'd moved to River Grove and had started something. Now it belonged to the town.

Despite my current fears, that made me feel good.

Chapter Sixteen

To get back to the bakery quickly, since I'd been gone almost a half an hour during a busy time, Biga and I ran back on the trail. He pulled on the leash, looking back at me, wide-eyed, enjoying the chase.

When we got to the cutoff to the alley, we slowed down. It was a little after 1 p.m.

I picked Biga up and walked up the back steps. The walk and the conversation with Reggie had refreshed me. Customer chatter and the clinking of plates and cups filtered into the back room.

Maeve was at the industrial mixer, churning brioche dough. She was singing to herself, with one headphone on, the other off, so she could hear if anything was needed up front.

She looked up. "It got busier as soon as you left. Beck will be happy to see you."

After setting Biga up in his pen, I washed my hands then slipped my apron over my head and went out front. Beck had just taken an order and Tyler and Elise were busily assembling a to-go lunch for a family of four, who had just stepped over to the pickup station to wait. There was a line of six people.

Beck put her hand to her chest and mouthed *thank you* when she saw me. I started taking orders, feeling a lot better than I had a half hour ago.

I took lunch orders, coffee orders and even handed out two job applications. As I just discovered, you never knew when you'd need replacements. The wonderful thing about today was, everyone coming into the bakery knew it was our opening day, and they were excited to be there. It felt like a party.

Janet from Clip n' Curl raved about the new place because there was now an option for lunch downtown that wasn't the corner store.

"You're my lunch spot now, Gracie," she said, as she bussed her dishes in the bin. "You're close by and way better than a stale wrapped sandwich."

After an hour, the lunch crowd thinned, and most people in line wanted espresso drinks and pastries. After the craziness of the lunch crowds eased, I saw Elise and Tyler visibly relax.

At 2:20 p.m., the end of our day was in sight. Beck walked through the dining area and gave the few people at the tables a friendly warning that we were closing soon.

I was still energized and smiling when a tall, unfamiliar man and a woman around my age came up and ordered cappuccinos and scones. The woman had big puffy lips, the kind that don't come naturally. My friend Elana would spot them a mile away.

I took their order and asked where they'd heard about the bakery.

The two exchanged a quick glance. "We are from—San

Franci-sco," the man said with an accent. "Also, we would like to pay in cash."

Suddenly I heard the voice of Maura Piccelli in my head. *If you see unfamiliar faces in the bakery....*

I scrambled to come up with a response, even as nausea roiled in my stomach. I felt dizzy. If these were the dissidents, and they used a credit card, we'd have a record of the transaction and a key to their identity.

"Unfortunately, we can only take digital payments right now," I said, firmly and cheerfully. "We're having a problem with the system. I'm sorry. You'll have to use the card reader."

The two looked at each other again and exchanged a stream of words I didn't understand. I swore I heard the name *Morrison*—or was it just my imagination? The man raised his eyebrows. The woman behind him smiled. I gulped.

"There is no other way? the man asked stiffly. "We are unable to pay with a card at this time."

"There isn't." I shook my head. "I'm sorry."

The two left the line and exited the front door, whispering to each other excitedly. They looked a little too happy to have had their form of payment rejected.

Soon the remaining diners at the tables got up to leave, still chatting on their way out.

At 2:30 p.m., Beck went up to the front door and flipped the Laughing Loaf sign over to the snoozing loaf.

"We're closed!" She said, taking a deep breath. "Gosh, guys. What a first day!"

Then, with a garbled cry to the rest of the staff that I suddenly felt sick, I stumbled into the back room and pulled open the door of the women's restroom. I closed it and turned the lock, my heart pounding.

I was glad I'd tucked my burner phone into my apron earlier.

I turned the water on in the sink to cover my voice then pulled the toilet cover down and sat. I pressed to dial the agents.

Maura answered after one ring in her firm, staccato voice.

"Tell me what's going on."

I spoke as quietly as I could.

"A man and a woman I'd never seen just came into the bakery and tried to pay in cash. Spoke in a language I didn't recognize—maybe a Slavic language. They may or may not have said the name *Morrison*." I stopped to catch my breath. "I told them we only accepted electronic payments. They said they could only pay in cash and left quickly."

"Give me descriptions. We'll be there in ten minutes. We'll get our local operative on it."

I closed my eyes and tried to picture the two customers in my mind.

"Both around my age. The man was tall and thin, short dark hair, with a mustache. Wearing black pants and a black jacket. The woman was about my height, long dark hair, blue eyes and really big lips. She was wearing a t-shirt and black cargo shorts."

"We're on it. Stay in the bakery. We'll contact local law enforcement and have them stationed outside."

When I heard the loud knock on the restroom door, I almost fell off the toilet.

"Gracie! Are you okay?" Beck sounded concerned. "We're worried about you."

I spoke in a weak voice. "I'm okay now. I thought I had to throw up." I stood up, feeling a little dizzy, and turned off the water faucet. "I'll be out in a minute."

I flushed the toilet and looked at myself in the mirror. My face was deathly pale. I wasn't trying for that effect, but it would probably convince the staff I'd really been sick.

I walked out of the bathroom on shaky legs.

"Gracie, please sit down." Beck led me to my office chair and made me sit. "Maeve, can you bring her some water?"

Maeve rushed to the tap and filled a glass. I saw Elise and Tyler in the doorway, looking anxious. Rose came over and stood by me.

"It's been a hell of a day for us all. And you're still dealing with Saturday's shock. Not a wonder you're feeling sick, Gracie." Maeve handed me the glass.

I took a sip and closed my eyes. I leaned back in my cushy chair. The water—and the fact that our crazy opening day was over—started to calm me down.

Beck pulled up a stool from the metal table and sat next to me. She put a hand on my shoulder. "You don't have to stay, Gracie. If you're still feeling sick, go home. We'll be fine. We know what to prep for tomorrow."

At this point, I was feeling better and had no intention of going home. Going through my usual prep and cleanup routine would keep me calm and centered.

I worried about my dad at home, but I trusted that Maura, Jeremy, or the local operative would keep an eye on our house. Right now, I was safest here.

"I'm fine now. I'll finish the water and then get up." I called to the lunch crew, who were bringing bread and condiments back to the fridge. "Tyler and Elise, go ahead and leave once you've cleaned up. Thanks for a great job today."

Elise smiled and Tyler gave me a thumbs up. They took off their aprons and put them in the bin, then went out to their cars parked in the alley. After they left, I got up and made sure the back door was locked.

Once Maeve turned the music on, I started to feel normal again. Beck, Maeve and Rose were singing along and telling stories about the day's highlights. I went out to the dining area to wipe down tables and bring in the tubs of bussed dishes.

When I looked through the front window, I saw the chief, wearing a bucket hat and sunglasses, hunched over one of the outside tables, reading a book and nursing probably the same coffee we'd made for him this morning. It made me laugh.

He was a law enforcement presence, and he probably did have a gun on him.

I suppose if someone did try to break into the bakery, he would be—well, our first line of defense.

Chapter Seventeen

"Thanks to Gracie's detailed descriptions, we know who the two people were in the bakery today." Maura spoke to us in a hushed voice in my dad's study that night.

"Both of them are in SABRE, the group looking for the pipeline codes."

Jeremy pulled out two photographs. I recognized the woman right away. "This is Zofia Zbirak, a high-ranking member of SABRE."

I recognized the man in the photo though here he didn't have a moustache. Maybe it was the quality of the copy, but he'd looked a lot younger in person. "And this is Henryk Volkov. He's in exile from Satrovania after spending time in prison there for anti-government activities."

"What are they trying to achieve by taking the pipeline down?" I asked, genuinely curious as to why shutting down a pipeline would be important to their cause. I suppose it would give them bargaining power, but if someone took away my ability to heat my house or drive my car, I'd be a hell of a lot less sympathetic to their cause.

"It's pretty simple. They want to bring the country to a standstill." Jeremy sat forward in his seat, his hands clasped in front of him. "They think that will get everyone to listen to them."

I took a deep breath and tried to chill out, after my busy and challenging day. "And they think *I* have the codes."

Maura and Jeremy exchanged glances, something I was getting very tired of.

Just say words, guys. Great that you know something, but please share it with me.

Maura took over. "The problem with SABRE is that they paid Ben for the codes. They never received them. They're blaming *you* for reneging on the deal."

I slumped down in my chair. Last year, it had been Russian spies trying to track down plans for a new fighter plane, which Ben had hidden in one of Biga's toys right before his arrest. The two men had stalked my friend Elana and me through The Riverside trying to get them and had finally ended up at my bakery, holding me hostage for the plans.

Now this. I wanted to cry because this was happening on the same day as the reopening of my bakery-- messing up what would have otherwise been a wonderful day.

There was a lump in my throat, but I couldn't cry. I'd been up since 4 a.m. I was too tired.

"Where are Volkov and Zbirak now?" I leaned my head against the back of the chair, exhausted.

"We now know the car they're driving—an old blue Chevy Malibu." Jeremy pulled another photo, a blurry one, from his envelope, then an enlargement of the license plate. "There's an APB out for the car, but no spottings yet. They may have figured out we're on to them. They may also have sympathetic supporters in the area."

"Gracie, we're hearing from our sources," Maura looked at me directly. "Volkov and Zbirak are telling the organization they've located you and confirmed your identity."

Jeremy leaned forward in his seat. "Satrovania is tiny, but it's in a strategic area in the Balkans. Our government has given Satrovania foreign aid to try to keep the country stable. But the country has an antiquated class structure, which is what SABRE wants to change."

"How desperate are these two people?" My father asked nervously. The fact that I'd come face to face with the dissidents seemed to have made a big impact on him. "Would they resort to violence?"

"Their group has in the past," Maura said. "They broke into the imperial palace and kidnapped the king's ten-year-old son, Prince Adalmi. He was released unharmed after negotiations with SABRE. At that point, Volkov and Zbirak were smuggled out of the country."

If Volkov and Zbirak had found me—did they have help from Barb? Had she been snooping around my office to try to figure out who I was and if I had the codes?

"Do you know if my employee, Barb D'Amato, had anything to do with the dissidents finding me?"

Jeremy tilted his head. "None of our contacts mentioned that name. She could have been recruited to find out if you were Ben's wife. They could have paid her to find out if Gracie Markley is Grace Morrison. Then, when they came today, they confirmed it for themselves."

This hit me hard, as I thought about the possibility that Barb had been recruited to get a job at The Laughing Loaf, to snoop around my office and confirm my identity. Had she gotten a job with us just to spy on me? Or had they approached her after we'd hired her?

"Could Barb have been killed once she'd given them the information?" I asked. "To wipe out their trail?"

Jeremy looked around for a treat of some kind, and his face brightened as he saw the plate of bright purple macarons. He took one. "That is typically not the group's *modus operandi*," he said. "Though they have gotten more desperate."

"All of this is speculation," Maura said impatiently, waving her hand. "We haven't heard of this woman or any ties she could have to SABRE. It's unfortunate that she was shot, but local authorities will deal with that. Jeremy and I are here to protect you and your father from the dissidents. We're sure that Volkov and Zbirak will be back. They want those codes."

"Tomorrow, we'll have surveillance at the bakery," she continued. "Another agent in our office will be stationed in the front, and your police chief has promised us coverage in the alley."

She nodded to my dad. "The operative will keep an eye on your house, John."

Jeremy slipped the photos back into his briefcase. "Both of you, call us, if you see these two again or see anything that seems suspicious."

We walked the agents to the front door. The meeting was reassuring in some ways. But the dissidents hadn't received what they paid for. They were angry, and I couldn't blame them.

I knew what it was like to be let down by Ben.

Chapter Eighteen

After he and I rehashed the details of our meeting with the agents, my father went back to his study to read. He was nervous after the meeting, though he didn't admit it. He told me he had a sudden desire to read about string theory.

When Nate made his usual call at 9, I was almost asleep.

"You sound exhausted, Gracie," Nate said with a quiet chuckle. "And I don't blame you. Sam told me the bakery was swamped today. A line going down the street before you opened."

Sam and Beck were next-door neighbors to Nate. He often heard about bakery goings-on from Sam, who'd become his close friend.

"I know. I was shocked." I sat up and rubbed my eyes. Biga looked up at me, annoyed that I'd moved and disturbed him. "A lot of people mentioned they were looking forward to the opening, but I didn't expect that many. I'm pretty wiped out."

He paused, then spoke quietly. "Beck told Sam that you got sick today after closing. She's worried about you."

I sighed. "Well, sort of. Something happened at the end of the day. But I don't feel comfortable talking about it on the phone."

"Do you want me to come over?"

As soon as he asked, tears began rolling down my face. I really wanted him to come over. I was tired, not just tired after a long day of work, but tired of spies and foreign dissidents coming after me. Tired of two-and-a-half years of living with the consequences of my life with Ben.

"I would really like that," I said, my voice shaky.

Fifteen minutes later, he was at the front door, backpack slung over his shoulder. I saw him through the peephole first because I couldn't be trusting today, not after what happened.

I let him in and locked the door.

"Would you like some brandy?" I asked. My dad had left the bottle out on the dining room table. He'd needed a snifter tonight after our meeting.

"Just a little."

I poured us each a glass and we sat down on the sofa.

"You want to tell me what happened?" He asked after he took a sip of his brandy, his light blue eyes studying my face.

I'd told him about the dissidents last week, so he knew the story. I told him about Volkov and Zbirak at the bakery. About my fears that the dissidents had paid Barb to confirm that I was *the* Grace Morrison.

And what the agents had told me about SABRE paying and not receiving the codes from Ben, who'd told them *I* had them.

The changes in Nate's face were subtle as I talked.

Something shifted under the surface of his face, his lips tightened. His jaw became rigid. A coldness came over his eyes until they flashed like they were made of steel. I had seen this look once. When his brother Nico had been killed behind the bakery a year and a half ago.

He said it quietly, almost in a whisper, but it shook me. "I hate him."

I swallowed and closed my eyes. I didn't like crying in front of people. I was the child of two Brits, who'd modeled the stiff-upper-lip attitude for me. But now my upper lip was wobbly, and I couldn't stop it. I leaned against Nate, and he held me, while I sunk my face into his chest, letting it absorb the tears and heaving.

We didn't talk after that. He didn't ask me how I was feeling or tell me everything was going to work out. He held me without talking. He kissed my head a few times.

I must have fallen asleep, because when I woke up, I was on the sofa, covered with a blanket, a pillow under my head. He was lying in my dad's recliner, which he'd pulled out. My dad adored Nate so much, he was probably the only person he'd be fine with using his personal reclining throne. Biga was curled up on Nate's stomach.

I set the alarm on my phone to sleep two more hours—until I had to get up at 4 a.m.

I got up, kissed Nate's forehead, and spread a quilt over him, then went back to the sofa and slept a deep, dreamless sleep.

When my alarm went off, I got up, rubbed the dried-tear detritus from my eyes and went to take a shower. I dressed and made coffee. When I came back into the living room, Nate was putting the recliner back in its dad-approved position, and the quilt was neatly folded.

"What can I help with?" He asked, with a warm smile.

"Can you get the Laughing Loaf aprons out of the dryer and put them in that basket on the washer? Then set them next to the front door."

"You got it. What about Biga? Where's the crate?"

"In the hallway. He'll probably do whatever *you* say, so just ask him to get into the crate. If he won't, throw in a treat and shut the door really fast."

Nate got busy, and soon the basket of clean aprons was by the door. Biga went into his crate without the use of a treat.

I put on my shoes, poured coffee for both of us and sat down at the table for a minute. Nate joined me.

"The chief will be staked out behind the bakery today. And the agents are monitoring the front door and keeping a watch for the couple's car." I took a gulp of coffee, willing the caffeine to get my brain in gear. "I feel better today. It'll be busy again, and that will keep my mind off things."

He nodded, a look of relief in his eyes. "If you want, I can stay here with your dad," he said.

"I know dad would love the conversation and a game of chess, but you don't have to. The agents said the local operative is keeping an eye on the house."

His eyes widened. "Do you know who this local operative is yet?"

"I have my suspicions, but I'm crossing Reggie off the list. He didn't seem to know about the SABRE threat."

Nate shook his head and smiled. "Too bad. Reggie as a government agent would have been awesome."

Nate helped me carry out the aprons, my tote bag, and Biga's crate and loaded the back of the Subaru.

Before I got in, I hugged him. "I needed you last night. I can't believe, after everything bad that's happened, I have you."

His mouth twisted up, as he tried not to smile but ended up smiling. I loved when he did that.

"You do, Gracie. You do have me."

Chapter Nineteen

When I pulled into the alley that morning at 4:30 a.m., there was a car parked right next to the bakery's back steps.

I was ready to pull out my burner phone and call the agents when I saw the insignia on the door and realized it was the River Grove PD's squad car.

I sighed with relief as I saw the chief in the driver's seat. He nodded and tapped the horn.

I waved back and went up the stairs. I unlocked the back door and immediately turned on all the lights in the bakery. I poked my head out the back door and gave the chief a thumbs-up. I texted him:

> If you need coffee and breakfast, text or knock!

Then I launched into my prep routine. I checked on my bread and cinnamon roll doughs in the fridge and took a peek at Maeve's brioche loaves in the proofer. We'd need the bread for the lunch crew. I checked the front counter, making sure all the options were in the syrup rack and the fridge was full of regular and alternative milks for the coffee drinks.

Out the front windows, the star on the animated Spinnetti's Sparkletown Cleaners sign sent out a shower of golden neon sparks into the early morning darkness.

The sparks illuminated the hood of the agents' shiny black truck, parked on the street in front of the bakery. I saw a phone light up in the driver's seat.

I was protected, behind and in front. The tight muscles in my neck and back began to relax. I put a playlist on and got on with my morning duties.

Beck came in the back door, her face full of worry. "Are you feeling better, Gracie?"

"A lot better." I nodded. "I think Barb's murder and yesterday's excitement got to me. It's all been... a lot."

"Oh, gosh. It has. Opening day was crazy. My nieces and nephews can't talk about anything but the bakery now. They're bugging my brothers to bring them back. They loved those cookies." Beck laughed. "Though my sisters-in-law were not happy with the amount of sugar they ate. They said the kids were bouncing off the walls."

I pictured feral mountain children scrambling through the house, running into the walls like a fleet of Roomba vacuums. It made me laugh, which I needed.

Beck set down a basket of eggs from the chickens she and Sam raised and began loading them into the rack in the fridge. "I saw the chief in the squad car out back. Is that for, like, crowd control or something?"

"Maybe," I said, noncommittally. "We did make a scene with that huge line. That doesn't happen in River Grove very often."

Beck grabbed a clean apron from the basket. "Or he could be investigating Barb's death," She dropped it over her head and tied the back. "Have you heard anything else about the case?"

"The chief hasn't said anything to me. Which is unusual."

I'd thought about Barb's death. But I hadn't heard any news from him or Mayor C. If the chief was going to be conveniently stationed behind the bakery this morning, I'd go ask him about it. I'd hoped to hear some kind of confirmation last night from Maura and Jeremy that Barb had been involved with SABRE, but no such luck.

At 6 a.m., Rose and Maeve came in the back door, donned their aprons and washed up. Rose had proven herself with the beignets yesterday. She got to work slicing the dough into squares as if she'd been doing it for months.

"I guess we have police protection now?" Maeve commented as she started pulling loaf pans from the proofer. "With what happened to Barb, that makes sense. Have you heard anything else about her case?"

"I need to check in with him today," I said. For my sanity, and to keep from obsessing about it, I needed to find out more.

"I'm glad there's somebody back there keeping an eye out," Rose said, placing dough squares onto a tray. "Especially when we come to work in the dark."

I sighed to myself, glad that there weren't any further questions about why the chief was on a stakeout at our back entrance.

I set the Laughing Loaf Joke of the Day on its stand on the counter.

Laughing Loaf Joke of the Day
Did you hear about the sensitive burglar?
He takes things personally.

Today, we opened at 7:30 a.m. to a shorter line. The beignets sold out within a half an hour. I told Beck she'd need to make a sign for the display case—telling customers that the sweet pillowy treats were limited to a half a dozen per customer.

At 8:30 a.m., when the chief and Mayor C usually came in for their morning public safety meeting, I only saw Mayor C. She strode in purposefully in her River Grove *A Small Town with Big Trees* t-shirt, a backpack over her shoulder, and ordered her coffee. Then she took a seat at her and the chief's new public safety meetup spot. She opened her laptop and began typing. She periodically stopped, sat back in her seat, and frowned at the screen. I really wanted to know what she was working on, but I was too busy taking orders at the counter to do anything about it. It was slightly less busy than the day before, but I still couldn't leave my post.

But when the mayor was still at her table an hour later, pounding away at her laptop, and the line of customers had died down, I asked Maeve if she'd cover the counter for fifteen minutes so I could take a break.

She nodded approvingly after I asked. "After your bout with the toilet yesterday, it's good to see you doing some self-care. Take your time. The brioche won't be done proofing for another half hour."

It was more snooping than self-care, but I flashed her a smile. "Thanks."

I grabbed a bottle of water from the fridge and went out to the dining area.

"I'm not used to seeing you in here by yourself, Corinne. Mind if I join you?"

The mayor looked annoyed at first, then gestured for me to take a seat.

"You saw Dave out in back. He says he's concerned that criminal elements are using the alley to cut through town. He thinks that's what happened to Barb—she was in the alley at the wrong time and got shot. Maybe she saw a deal going down."

So now River Grove's seedy back alleys were a hotbed of drug dealing?

The chief had spun quite a tale to avoid telling the mayor about the dissidents' visit to the bakery.

I didn't know what to say to this.

"Do *you* think that's what happened to Barb?"

The mayor paused for a moment. "I don't think the chief is being honest with me."

The chief and the mayor had a falling out last year, over the arrest of someone she thought was innocent of the murder of rockstar Noah Thornton Bell. The weeks that the chief and the mayor weren't talking to each other were painful to me. It was like seeing your parents fight. I didn't want it to happen again.

I wanted to hear what the mayor thought had happened to Barb, since she'd actually known the woman.

"Corinne, you said you suspected Barb might have done something illegal, or at least ill-advised, to get money. Any more ideas about what that might have been?"

The mayor zipped opened her backpack and pulled out a sheet of paper with some notes on it.

"This morning I talked to Amora Davis, who works at Boulder Creek Credit Union. We're in the hiking club together." The mayor took a quick glance at her phone, which had just lit up with a notification. "She told me Barb came in on Saturday around 10 a.m. to deposit a cashier's check. The check was for $10,000."

I looked over at Maeve, who was taking an order from a

young mom with a baby in a stroller. No one else in line. "Seriously? Did she tell Amora what it was for?"

"She told her it was for 'valuable services.' She wouldn't tell her anything else." The mayor shook her head. "Not long after that, Barb was dead."

The money had to be connected with Barb's death. For that amount, Barb must have provided *extremely* valuable services. Perhaps she'd obtained info for a couple of desperate foreign dissidents, who then made sure she wouldn't tell anyone who they were.

"Did you tell the chief about this?"

"Not yet." The mayor closed her laptop and started returning it and the papers to her backpack. "He's been out in the squad car. He seems to be taking a different angle on the case."

"Corinne, you guys need to talk. The chief might be a little distracted, but you need to tell him about this. Now you know something was going on with Barb—this wasn't just a random shooting in the alley."

The mayor pressed her lips together and nodded. "I knew it wasn't. Barb had a string of bad luck, and she was trying to deal with it the best she could. I want to find her killer." She slid some papers into her backpack and zipped it up. "And I'd like to you to help me. Barb's former assistant manager Carlene is meeting me here in a few minutes. I want to ask her some questions about Barb's situation. I'd like you to join me."

"Um, *what*?" I looked around at my crowded bakery, which was going to keep me busy for the foreseeable future. I thought about the two dissidents lurking out there, waiting to hunt me down, for something I didn't have.

"Barb was your employee. You investigate murders all the time," Mayor C said sharply, as if saying it more loudly and clearly would persuade me to drop everything for an investigation. "Isn't it the *least* you could do for Barb, Gracie?"

I tried to figure out if I could spare another ten minutes to sit in on the conversation with Carlene.

In the meantime, Elise called me over to the counter to tell me we were out of flatbread. I made a run to the back room to bring out a tray of fresh-from-the-oven flatbread for wraps.

When I returned to the front area, a blond woman in her forties had joined Mayor C.

The woman pulled out a chair and took a seat across from the mayor.

The mayor called me over.

"Gracie, this is Carlene McCaffrey. Barb's former assistant manager at Mangia Mama."

The petite woman with long, bleached platinum hair looked up at me, her eyes red rimmed. I did not have any time to spare today, but I did want to meet the woman and ask her about Barb.

"I'm sorry for your loss, Carlene." I took a seat at the table hoping this would be a short conversation. "You'd worked with Barb almost from the start of her business, right?"

Carlene nodded. She took a tissue out of her purse and daubed at her eyes.

"Since she first set up the shop in Boulder Creek. Barb was a wonderful woman," she said, with a catch in her voice. "And my friend."

"Did you stay in touch after she shut down Mangia Mama?" I asked. "Was she looking for a new space?"

Carlene sniffed. "Well, she didn't talk much about it, but I think so. She told me she wanted to take the business in a new direction, and she was sure she could get some funding." She shook her head. "Barb was always an optimist."

"Did she say where she was looking for funding?" Mayor C asked. "Was she looking for a loan? An investor?"

The woman brushed her hair off her face with a delicate wave of her hand. "She didn't say. I wish I could be more helpful."

"How recently did you talk to her?" I asked, curious about Barb's state of mind before the day of her murder.

Carlene closed her eyes as she thought about it. "It must have been Thursday. Yes, that's it. She left a voice mail for me that day."

I studied the woman's face. "What did she say?"

Mayor C leaned across the table. "And how did she sound?"

Carlene looked between the two of us, trying to figure out who to answer first.

"She told me she had a lead on some money," she said quietly. "But it was weird. She sounded scared."

I looked up to see Maeve making a dash to the back room. Beck was now at the front counter, filling in for me, and I saw a new line of customers forming. I groaned.

"I'm sorry—duty calls. Good to meet you, Carlene, and thanks for talking to us."

So Barb had sounded scared on her message to Carlene. It was becoming clear to me. Barb must have had been working with the dissidents.

And when they'd gotten what they wanted from her, they'd gotten rid of her.

Chapter Twenty

We started lunch service at 11 a.m., with Elise and Daisy at the counter. Tyler had an exam for his summer session class at San Jose State. The two young women naturally tag-teamed with each other on their duties. They seemed more outgoing and in better spirits together. Strange how different pairings of people can change the mood and dynamic of a place. When I went out to work the espresso machine for Rose, I saw the difference. Customers chatted with each other and waited in line more patiently. Daisy laughed and smiled more, lightly bantering with customers as she took their orders.

Should I work with the mayor in her investigation?

Unlike Elise and Daisy today, the mayor and I didn't always have a great working relationship. I did want to figure out who killed Barb. If not for Barb, whom I still resented a bit for her snooping, then for the idea of keeping River Grove safe.

After Rose came back from lunch, I went to the back room and used my scorer to create a pretty leaf pattern on my country sourdough loaves, which were ready for baking.

We were going through so much more bread now that we served lunch. Our batches of sandwich breads were bigger now, with brioche and flatbread being the two most popular. It helped that the flatbread for wraps was quicker to make. Since Maeve knew Rafal's recipe well, she churned them out at a fairly quick pace.

After putting the country loaves in the oven, I set the timer and slid it into my apron pocket. I'd have a quick conversation with the chief if the squad car was still there.

As I opened the back door, I saw he'd backed the car into a parking spot on the alley, which gave him a clear view of the bakery's back door. I waved as I headed toward the car.

I tapped on his window.

"Any action going on out here?"

The chief had a pile of forms on a clipboard that he was going over, and his tablet was open and lying on the dashboard. He took a sip from a Laughing Loaf cup.

"Who brought you coffee?" I'd gotten busy and completely forgotten about it.

"Beck brought it out to me, along with an egg on toast." He shrugged. "She wanted to thank me for keeping you all safe."

"She's a lot nicer than I am."

The chief chuckled. "Well, you have your moments, Gracie."

I had to get back inside, since things were getting busy for lunch.

"My staff wants to know how things are going with the Barb investigation. Any updates?"

"One thing." The chief picked up the tablet and looked at a report displayed on the screen. "The bullet that killed Barb was likely shot from a Luger. An old, German-made pistol known for its accuracy. It's not the kind of gun you see around here."

"Which means what?" I asked. "The killer was some-body from out of the area?"

Or maybe out of the country.

"The killer was probably a professional. Barb died instantly, according to the coroner."

That was something to be thankful for. Barb didn't deserve to be killed, and at least she didn't suffer.

I frowned at the chief.

"Earlier today, you told the mayor that the alley was being used as a thoroughfare in town, by 'criminal elements.' And that's why you're on watch back here."

The chief rubbed his face and looked at me. His eyes looked tired. "What the hell was I supposed to say, Gracie? That there were dissidents from another country hunting you down? I can't tell her the truth."

"Okay, but what you did tell her was pretty far-fetched. The mayor's a smart lady. She knew Barb, and she wants some answers about her death. Have you talked to her today? She said Barb made a big bank deposit that morning, before she was killed."

He stared at me. "Are you serious?" He took out his phone and started to make a call.

"I just had a conversation with her in the bakery. We also talked to Barb's assistant manager, Carlene McCaffrey. She said Barb sounded scared of something."

I stood on the steps, because, yes, I am a snoop. I heard the mayor answer on the speaker phone in the squad car. Maybe I shouldn't have told the chief these things, but the mayor wasn't going to talk to him without a nudge.

At least they were talking. I heard their conversation. The mayor was telling him about the deposit at the credit

union and what Amora Davis had told her—then speculating where Barb had gotten the money. She shared
Carlene's comment that Barb had found a new source of
money for the business.

The chief interrupted with a lot with questions.

I had questions, too. But before I was tempted to listen
any longer, I opened the back door and went back to work.

Chapter Twenty-One

The only problem with lunch service that day was that we ended up running out of flatbread completely.

For the last hour of the day, customers ordered sandwiches instead—reluctantly.

It wasn't that people didn't like our usual breads, but after our opening, word had gotten around town, and flatbread was having a moment.

It was made the same day, sometimes still warm when the customer received it, and was softer and fluffier than store-bought wraps. We'd just have to make more.

I thanked Daisy and Elise as they left and complimented them on their rapport with customers. I made a note to schedule them on more shifts together.

When we closed for the day, the remaining staff gathered in the back room, all of us on an adrenaline high. We turned on the music and started chatting about how the day went.

"Elise kept asking for more flatbread," Maeve said.

"That and brioche. I'll convert the recipes to higher quantities."

"Things went more smoothly today," Rose said, thoughtfully. "We didn't have quite as many customers, but we still had a lot. The systems seem to be working. And we're not as nervous, maybe."

Rose's observations lately about the workings in the bakery showed some potential for management. I tucked that away for future reference.

"I know I'm not. I had a lot more fun today," Maeve said. "And Elise and Daisy rock."

"I thought so, too!" Beck added.

As everyone got to work on prep for tomorrow, the three of them started talking about going over to The Riverside for drinks after work. Maeve had introduced Beck to this before the renovation. Beck had her first experience with drinking alcohol, and the two had bonded as friends. They both encouraged Rose to join them.

After they left out the back door, giggling and talking, I watched them until they reached their cars. Brad Castro had relieved the chief in the squad car and the deputy was sitting in the driver's seat, playing what looked like a hand-held video game. I waved and he waved back, so he must have been paying at least some attention to his duties.

I felt a little left out not joining my staff, but the feeling passed. I was the boss and at least ten years older than all of them. I was happy they got along so well. I wanted Beck to have some fun time with girlfriends before she plunged into the responsibilities of having a family.

I sat down at my desk and went over revenue for today and for yesterday—which had been phenomenal. Beck had counted 244 customers yesterday. I'd been a little skeptical, but looking at our totals, it added up.

I sat down on the floor in the pen next to Biga, who was looking bored and ready to go home. He'd pushed the terrifying interactive toy into the far corner of the pen. He crawled into my lap, and I scratched his back.

"You've been so good, Biga. It must be hard for you to smell all the food and not be able to get near it."

Typical of a dog, Biga began licking my hand and my face. *It's okay, Best Human Ever! All is forgiven!*

I packed up our stuff in my tote bag, then went up to check the front counter area. Everything looked tidy, all surfaces wiped down. The display case had been cleared out, ready to be loaded up tomorrow morning.

It was still light and fairly sunny, even as the sun dipped lower and lower toward the tops of the redwoods. Another agent, Hawk, whom I remembered Maura introducing me to, was in the shiny black truck. He nodded when he saw me. I waved back.

Just before I headed to the back room to get Biga and my bag, I saw something white on the floor near the door. I thought it was a napkin from the dispenser at first.

It was an envelope.

Handwritten in capital letters, it read:

MRS GRACE MORRISON

My heart pounded, as that name brought up a vivid stream of memories, everything I'd been through both in Seattle and here.

Was it from the dissidents? Should I wait to open it?

I went to my office and dug in my tote bag for my purse. I fumbled for the burner phone and pulled it out.

I pushed the contact number.

"What's going on, Gracie?" Maura's taut voice answered.

"Someone slipped an envelope under the front door. It's

addressed to Grace Morrison." I gulped. My thumb and finger had a vise-like grip on the corner of it. I wanted to keep it safe. I also wanted to touch as little of it as possible.

"Hawk's going to stay in the truck on alert. I'll be there in ten minutes. We'll open it then."

I made myself a cup of tea, then went back to the table where the envelope sat. I sipped my tea and stared at it, while reassuring myself that Hawk was still stationed in his truck out front.

When had the envelope been dropped into the mail chute? I'd been in the room maybe fifteen minutes before that and hadn't seen a envelope on the floor.

I waited, as I thought of Beck, Maeve, and Rose laughing and eating appetizers at The Riverside. I'm glad they were there, having fun, not seeing me—or the look of fear on my face.

Maura appeared at the front door, not dressed in any of her country, cutesy outfits, but just in black sweats, Nike running shoes and a black t-shirt. Her hair was pulled back into a sloppy ponytail pinned up by a plastic claw clip. She looked like a soccer mom or someone you'd pass by in an aisle at the grocery store without really noticing. Maybe this was how she dressed at home.

I let her in, then immediately locked the door.

Maura slipped on some gloves and handed me a pair. We sat down at the table. She picked up the envelope and slit it open with a tool she'd pulled out of her purse.

She laid the letter out on the table.

Mrs Grace Morrison

You and your husband promised us oil pipeline access codes two-and-a-half years ago after receiving our payment of 50,000 US dollars.

It is time to give us the codes we paid for. We do not want to hurt you, but we will if you do not produce for us these codes.

We now know where you are, where you and your father live, and where you work. You can no longer hide from SABRE.

You will meet us at Shark Fin Cove Friday at 12 p.m. You will come by yourself with the codes, or we break this deal. Then you will pay in a very different way. We will know if you bring law enforcement with you.

Henryk Volkov
SABRE
Freedom Force of Satrovania

I put my head down on the table. In a shocking turn of events, the stern, aloof Maura patted my arm to comfort me.

I sighed. I couldn't lift my head off the table.

"I don't have the access codes. I knew nothing about them. What do I tell them? Do I show up empty handed?"

"Gracie, last time Ben hid the plane schematic in one of Biga's toys." She raised her eyebrows. "It's not like Ben wanted to help Satrovania or SABRE in any way, we all know that. Once he got his money, he didn't care whether they got the codes or not. To him, the codes were an asset. He could get money for them from somewhere else. And we know how important money was to Ben. I want you to think. Is there any place he might have thought of to hide those codes?"

"I don't know." I rubbed my aching temples. My brain was too full: things to remember at the bakery, Barb's unsolved murder, and of course, fear. For my life, my dad's and Biga's.

Maura nodded. "He could have stashed them someplace for safekeeping. I want you to think. And you need to think fast. We have two days."

I sat up suddenly. "The note says they *know* where I am. What does that mean?"

Maura sat for a moment. Then she got up. "Where are you parked?"

I led her through the back door and out into the alley. Maura stalked over to my car and ran her hand underneath the back bumper. She tugged on something and came back with a small device in her hand.

"This is how they knew."

With a heavy sigh she approached Brad Castro in the River Grove Police Squad car. She tapped on the driver's side window, and Brad looked up from his video game. She showed her badge. Brad started the car and rolled down the window, a terrified look on his face.

"I need to check your back bumper, Deputy."

He nodded and gulped.

She ran her hand underneath the squad car's bumper and pulled out a similar device.

She brought both devices up to Brad's window and gave him a withering look. "GPS trackers. Be more diligent, deputy."

She and I went back into the bakery.

"That's how they'd know if you brought law enforcement. The SABRE organization is not particularly sophisticated, but they do have common sense."

As we headed for the front of the bakery, Maura asked if she could have a latte.

"It's been a long day. Jeremy and I have a couple of leads to follow up tonight. We think the two are still in the area, but we have no idea where."

I started up the espresso machine and prepared to make her a drink. While it was warming up, I went into the back room to grab a couple of sourdough starter chocolate chip cookies for her. Honestly, I had no idea what Maura's life was like outside of her time with my dad and me. She and Jeremy both kept that under wraps.

Was she married? Did she have kids? I didn't know, but today she looked tired and badly in need of chocolate chip cookies.

Going through the motions of making the latte helped me think.

Would Ben have hidden the codes somewhere? I could see where he would have hidden them in my things just to be vindictive. Hoping that would convince people I'd been in on the scheme with him.

I mixed in the steamed milk and poured it into the espresso in the cup. Then I plated the cookies and brought everything out to Maura.

"Thanks," she said crisply as I sat down. She took a bite of one of the cookies. Her eyes opened wide and she looked at me. "This is good."

I was still trying to think of where Ben could have stashed the codes. I could go through my work computer here and see what I could find. Maybe he'd copied something onto it.

He would have had the opportunity to since I'd taken

off with Biga and my small work bag the morning I'd left for the FBI office. I'd taken a laptop, but I'd left my desktop computer on my desk at home. Ben would have had access to it.

Or he could have stashed a USB stick or removable hard drive into anything else I'd left before he was arrested.

"Maura, I don't know where to start. He could have left it in anything that was still in our house that day before his arrest."

I looked out the front window, where the sun had just set, casting purple-grey shadows over the street. The agent's truck was still in front of the bakery.

"You keep thinking, Gracie." Maura had finished off her cookies and took one last swig of her latte. "I've got to go. If anything comes to you, let me know ASAP."

I let Maura out the front door. She gave a subtle nod to Hawk in the truck, then took off down the street in a light jog, looking as if she were late for picking up her kid from soccer practice.

I turned off the espresso machine and went through the bakery turning off lights. When I took the crate back to Biga's pen, he looked up at me with those big brown eyes as if he thought I'd completely forgotten about him. I picked him up and cuddled him first.

"I'm sorry, Biga boy. We're going home now."

I put him down and with one more sad look up at me, he crawled into the crate.

With a nod to Brad in the squad car, we left to go home and recover.

Chapter Twenty-Two

Dad was in the kitchen making dinner, which meant he was reheating chicken curry I'd made earlier in the week. He'd arranged a bagged salad from the grocery store in a bowl with some baby carrots, to prove he had the vegetable food group covered.

"Hard day, dear?" He called as I set the crate down and let Biga out. My face must have shown how overwhelmed I was. I flopped down onto the sofa.

"The dissidents definitely think I have the pipeline codes." I told him about the letter I'd received at the bakery. "Now they're saying if I don't hand them over Friday, someone gets hurt."

My father set the pot of curry back on the stove to heat up. He took two bottles of ale out of the fridge and came to sit down next to me.

"You don't have them." He was starting to look worried. "Do you?" He popped the caps off the bottles with an opener and handed me one.

"No. But then, I didn't think I had the schematics for the stealth fighter either. It's possible Ben might have hidden them in something of mine. I can't even think of where."

When I was married to Ben, my dad kept his opinions to himself. Sometimes I wished he would have spoken up. But then, as he told me once, sometimes when a parent disapproves of your partner, it pushes you closer to him. I tried to think of what I was like as a 22-year-old—around the age of Beck, Maeve, and Rose.

"Let's see." He took a sip of his ale. "Your computer? Your desk would have been there, too. Have you looked through the drawers—maybe under the drawers?"

I'd check the desk in my room later.

The evening was hot since we had no air conditioning at home, and the cool ale helped. I took another sip. My dad served dinner, a creamy yellow curry that tasted amazing— because, of course, I'd made it myself. We tossed out more possibilities for where Ben might have hidden the codes. My dad took a methodical approach to nearly everything in his life. Even if it made me impatient sometimes, his thoughts forced me to slow down and pay attention to details.

I missed Nate and looked forward to talking to him tonight, but I really wanted to brainstorm with Elana. She was my go-to for bouncing ideas around. I'd give her a call after dinner.

I took Biga out in the backyard and we had some chasing time. He'd been saving his energy up all day, so he had a bad case of the zoomies. By the time we headed back into the house, I felt like I'd run a half marathon.

I went into my room and texted Elana.

I need to brainstorm.

You available?

No immediate response. Elana, who constantly monitored her phone, usually got back to me within a minute or two. Either she and Kirk were doing a date night, or she was at a work event.

Following my dad's suggestion, I took all the drawers out of my desk and scoured their surfaces for any hidden USB sticks. I turned the desk around and searched the back. Then I carefully upended the thing so I could look over the bottom and back panels.

Nothing.

Tomorrow I'd do a thorough search on my computer at the bakery. It was five years old, and I'd had it at home in Seattle. It would be the most obvious place for Ben to store something. With everything going on in my life at the time, I hadn't done a great job of deleting old files. Other than all my photos of Ben.

At 9, Nate called, in a great mood because he'd gone through his photos from the Yosemite shoot and felt great about them.

"I'll send you some right now," he said, excitedly. "This is for a book about Yosemite, so they're not just birds. I know you like waterfalls, so these are for you."

"Aww, for me?"

The photos appeared in my texts. First was a beautiful wide sheet of water tumbling down a sheer cliff. A rainbow hovered in the mist surrounding it.

"This is Vernal Falls, on the Mist Trail. To get this view, you walk along a trail carved into the mountainside. It's like something out of *Lord of the Rings*, Gracie. Like when Aragorn and the hobbits are hiking through Misty Mountains. It's magical. You'd love it."

He sent another photo, an elegant, slender strand flowing down a mountainside dotted with trees and plants with bright orange flowers. "If you continue to hike up on that trail, you see this waterfall. But I have something else to show you. One's my shot, but the next one isn't—it's what the waterfall will look like in February."

He sent a photo of a slender, very tall waterfall gushing down the side of a massive, flat rock mountainside. It was probably the longest waterfall I'd ever seen. It was impressive just for its length.

"That's Horsetail Falls. Now this next photo I didn't take because it's July and this only happens once a year."

He sent a photo of the same waterfall, but the water had become a long orange strand tumbling down the rock face in a mist of fire. It was eerie and striking.

"This is The Firefall. It only happens in late February. The sunset hits the falls and makes it look—well, like a long stream of fire. Next year, I want to take this photo."

"It's stunning." I took in my breath. "It's unreal—"

"I want you to go with me, Gracie." The way he said it gave me chills. He said it with such gravity, it sounded like a proposal. I didn't know what to say. Especially right now when I was facing a meetup on Friday that could have disastrous consequences. I hoped I'd still be around in February.

I took a deep breath, as if I were inhaling hope.

"I would love to see it."

He was quiet for a minute or two. I knew he wanted to ask about the situation with the dissidents. It terrified him to know I was in danger. Last year, he backpacked in the Pacific Northwest by himself so he could think about whether he could be in a relationship with someone he could lose.

"Any updates on the dissidents?"

At this point in our relationship, I was telling him everything. He'd proven beyond a doubt that he could be trusted. And I couldn't be in a relationship with someone I couldn't tell the truth to. I'd already been in a relationship with someone who couldn't tell the truth to *me*.

I told him about the letter. It was a while before he spoke.

"You don't have the codes."

"Nope. At least I don't think so. Maura's telling me to look for them, since last fall I found the plane schematic on a USB stick inside Biga's toy. They think Ben wanted to offload them on me, to prove I was involved or to keep them handy in case he had a chance to sell them again. If you have any ideas about where I should look, I'm open to suggestions."

"I'm sure I don't think like Ben, but—"

"I'm sure, too," I said with a tired laugh.

"How about your baking stuff? Any equipment you had in Seattle. Cookbooks, pans, bread knives, or tools in boxes that maybe you haven't checked in a while."

"I do have some things I brought down in the move that I haven't used. I'll go through those."

"What happens if you can't find the codes?" His voice shook a little.

"The agents are trying to figure that out." I lay back on the bed and readjusted the phone. "I trust them—or at least, I have no other choice but to trust them. They were there outside the bakery today. The local operative is keeping an eye on our house."

"You mean Deputy Brad?" I thought I heard him snort.

"He was in the squad car until I left. Playing a Pokémon video game."

"That's just what he wants everyone to think. It's a great cover for an operative."

"The possibilities for the local operative are dwindling." I laughed.

"If he's the one, it's a brilliant ploy."

Chapter Twenty-Three

On Wednesday morning, I set out the Laughing Loaf Bakery Joke of the Day on its stand.

Laughing Loaf Joke of the Day
What did one plate say to the other?
Lunch is on me!

The staff was hyped up for another busy day on reopening week.

At least the ones who hadn't overindulged last night during girls night at The Riverside. Maeve said the three of them stayed out till 11 p.m. Rose asked if I had ibuprofen for a headache, and Maeve kept turning her head to yawn. Beck was her cheerful, bright-eyed self.

Nobody was waiting outside the door, no line. It looked like our only guests at the bakery were Hawk, parked discreetly a few cars down, and the chief, who was keeping watch in the alley. I still worried about Friday, but now, in the bakery, I felt safe.

As soon as we opened at 7:30 a.m., one customer came in. Jake Daniels walked through the door all smiles.

"G'morning, Gracie. I wanted to get something to celebrate Jeanne's birthday today."

"Oh, tell her happy birthday for me, Jake." I took a quick look at the display case. "What's her favorite pastry? She likes beignets, I remember."

His face lit up. "She *loves* beignets. Do you have the chocolate filled ones?"

"You're in luck. They're fresh out of the hot oil."

"Can you do a dozen and a half?"

I pointed to the sign on the display case that Beck had made: A person looking tearful that beignets were limited to six per customer.

"But if we consider this a catering order, I think it's fine. It's for your staff to celebrate her birthday?"

Jake nodded. I placed the beignets in a pink box then went back to find edible glitter. A dash of purple, Jeanne's favorite color, would be a nice touch. I lightly sprinkled some over the beignets then sealed the box up.

"Thanks, Gracie." Jake finished his payment at the pay station and left a large tip. "Jeanne's gonna love these."

I thought I might have a few minutes to check out my computer in the office, to search for any files Ben might have added. But ten minutes later, business picked up big-time and we were busy for the rest of the day—especially at lunch. There had been a mention of our new lunch service in the *Santa Cruz Sentinel*, so several customers had driven up from the coast.

The chief's daughter, Renee, came in during lunch, dressed in business casual. She looked like she'd taken a break from work. She walked around the bakery's front area, looking at the photographs. She approached me at the counter.

"My dad told me about your new place, and I had to come in and see for myself. Looks fantastic." She smiled and with her long wavy blond hair and the touch of sass in her smile, I saw how much Chloe resembled her. Suddenly she sobered. "How are you doing these days?"

I wondered if she knew why her father was on a stakeout in the alley.

I tightened my lips. "Things have been a little crazy."

She studied my face and nodded, with a look of sympathy. "Sorry, Gracie. I can only imagine."

What did she mean by that? Was she commenting on how busy we'd been at the bakery this week? The long process of renovation? Or had the chief said something to her about my situation?

Whichever it was, I just smiled and thanked her. I was reading too much into everything these days.

"You should try a wrap, Renee. They're excellent."

"I think I will," she said with a nod. "Thanks, Gracie."

With her loaf-shaping done, Maeve came up to work the counter, and I took a break to go back to my office.

I'd get a start on checking my big, aging warhorse of a computer for any sign of the pipeline access codes.

First, I ran my hand over the surface of my monitor, then along the computer tower itself. Nothing.

I sat down in my chair and started my file search, narrowing it down to that time, over two years ago, when I'd found out Ben's secret. I searched for files uploaded within a three-day range—right up to the day he was arrested.

The search listed ten files. As I scanned through them, most of them were from my tech job in software project management for my old employer, Sound Shore Systems.

But I opened each one anyway, just to make sure Ben hadn't renamed something important to make it look innocuous.

Each one was exactly what it looked like: lists of project schedules and product release dates.

The two final files had names I didn't recognize. I opened each one, to find that they were silly memes Ben had uploaded to my computer, thinking he was being funny. One was a picture of a chicken being plucked, with the headline: YOU MISSED YOUR PROJECT DEAD-LINE? YOU'RE NOW ON THE MENU.

Another one was a photo of a little boy and girl walking hand in hand up a very steep, narrow street. The caption read: *When you love someone, every walk is special.*

What the hell?

Was this how my self-obsessed, narcissistic ex felt about me? He certainly didn't act like it, and this did not sum up my feelings for him. It did, though, describe how I felt about Nate. I hated walking uphill (almost everyone knew that), but I'd do it with Nate in a minute if it was something he wanted. Because Nate truly cared about me. Time with him was always special.

So my computer held no access codes that I could find. Maybe Ben had been sneaky and put them in a hidden folder, which I'd check for later. But my gut told me I wouldn't find anything on the computer.

Before I went back to the front counter, I wanted to do an internet search. Would there be info on SABRE? Every-thing was searchable, so why not this group? I typed it in the Google search bar and found an entry on Wikipedia.

SABRE

A dissident group based in the small country of Satrovania, located in the Balkan region of Europe. SABRE [Satrovanian Movement for Liberty, Justice, and Equality] formed in 1986 in opposition to the country's 500-year-old monarchy led by the Petrov-Amirov family. In protest against the king's authoritative reign, SABRE has demanded freedom of speech and equal access to political power for all classes in Satrovanian society. With little progress in that area, SABRE was formed. The group has resorted to kidnapping the king's son, Prince Admiri, and various acts of sabotage and vandalism to bring attention to their cause. Because of Satrovania's strategic position in the Balkans, the Petrov-Amirov monarchy has received ongoing support from the United States and various European nations, who fear instability in the 63-square-mile nation.

As I read more, I saw examples of the monarchy's campaigns in the twentieth century to "re-educate" dissidents through what they called Truth Camps.

I was terrified of SABRE and what they might do to me Friday if I didn't show up with codes for their pipeline attack. But at least I understood their motives now. Volkov and Zbirak were fighting for greater freedom for their people. They were desperate to bring attention to their cause.

Before I went back to work the counter, I pulled my phone out and checked it. Elana had left a message this morning.

Sorry to miss your text!

Kirk and I had a BlueSurf exec dinner in
Capitola. Let's brainstorm. Riverside at 7?

This worked for me. My dad and Mary Jo were making
dinner at our house.

Maybe Elana could give me some ideas on where to
look for the codes. I had to be careful what I told my friend,
though. She was like a magpie, picking up shiny bits of
gossip and redistributing them here and there.

She absolutely could not do that now.

At noon, when we were most crowded, Mayor C came
in and ordered a veggie hummus wrap, then went to grab a
seat near the window. A mom and her two rambunctious
toddlers were in the process of leaving the table. The dining
area was full.

The mom and kids could not leave fast enough for the
mayor. She stood a few feet away, looked up from her phone
at the woman and her squirmy children, and edged closer
and closer to the table. Right as they hurried out, she
swooped in to nab the spot.

She plunked herself down, took out her laptop, and
spread papers out on the table. When Elise called her name,
the mayor covered the papers with her backpack and went
to pick up her wrap.

The mayor was up to something. I hoped the chief had
talked to her about Barb's murder and she wasn't going off
on her own. If she had, well—I really wanted to hear what
she'd found out.

But I had a bakery to run. Lunch looked like it was
going to be our busiest time today.

Elise leaned over from the lunch counter.

"Gracie, we just ran out of flatbread again. Brioche is

out, too. Maeve says there's none coming out of the oven for the rest of the day."

"Then wraps are off the menu. Offer to use the same toppings on a sourdough or whole wheat sandwich."

"Okay," she said tentatively. She frowned, looking over at the customer she was going to have to tell this to. "I'll do that, but he's not going to be happy."

The customer wasn't happy with either choice, so he ended up leaving with coffee and a pastry.

As much as organic whole wheat was a hippie tradition in the Santa Cruz Mountains, we'd probably end up reducing the loaves of whole wheat bread we baked. Customers were skipping right past it to get their fluffy wraps and to order sandwiches on buttery brioche.

After about an hour, I saw Mayor C pack up her backpack. When she came to bus her plate and cup in the tub next to the front counter, I called her name.

"Corinne, can I come by City Hall to talk at 4:30?"

She nodded. "I'll be there. I've found out something I think you'll want to know."

Chapter Twenty-Four

After we closed for the day, Elise and Tyler cleaned up the lunch area and brought leftovers back to the industrial fridge.

"I've been here for four and a half hours. Why does it feel like ten?" Tyler groaned as he took a bottle of cold water from the fridge. He twisted off the top and glugged it down.

"An entire swarm came in for lunch," Maeve said. "It makes me wonder if we're a stop for some tour bus line."

"News has gotten around about The Laughing Loaf having a lunch service," I said. "The bloggers and newspapers that said good things about our bakery are letting people know we do lunch now. A few customers mentioned it."

"Oh yeah, Gracie." Beck turned around from a pan of tart shells that would become Strawberry Shortbread Tarts. "I answered the phone when you were out yesterday. Somebody from the *San Jose Mercury News* asked me a bunch of questions about our lunch menu and hours."

"Well, there you go." I smiled.

After doing prep for the next day, and wiping down the dining area, I asked Beck, Rose, and Maeve to lock up, since I needed to talk to Mayor C.

I peered out the back door. Brad was now keeping watch in the squad car in the alley.

I pinged Mayor C by text to ask if she could meet me on the back steps of City Hall since I needed to get Biga outside. He'd been incredibly patient. While I'd managed to take him out back for a few pee breaks, he needed to get out for a walk.

I got a typically curt response from our mayor.

fine

I put the leash on Biga and went out the front door, then locked it. Biga was thrilled to be outside.

I tapped on the window of the black truck as I passed it, to let Hawk know I was going over to City Hall.

He rolled down his window, took off his black glasses and a warm smile broke across his rugged face. "So this is Biga. Hey, big boy. He's a cute one, Gracie." Biga wiggled with delight and began wagging his tail.

"We're walking over to talk to the mayor on the back steps of City Hall. I'll be maybe 20 minutes."

"You want me to follow you?"

"I think we'll be fine. It's just across the street and in back."

"Jeremy called ten minutes ago and said they've had a possible sighting of Volkov in Monterey. I'll text you my number. If you have any problems, call. If I hear anything more, I'll let you know."

"Thanks, Hawk." Biga and I waited for a car to pass,

then ran across the street. We took a shortcut through the corridor between City Hall and Spinnetti's and came around at the back of city hall.

Mayor C was sitting on the steps, phone in hand and a notepad on her lap.

I stood while Biga found a place to pee in a nearby weed patch.

"Thanks for inviting yourself over, Gracie." From the looks of the circles under her eyes, she hadn't been sleeping well. "I've been frustrated with the progress on Barb's case. I did talk to the chief. He said the deposit Barb made was of interest. But he hasn't spent much time on the case. He says he's had to work on something else. Of course, he didn't bother to tell me what."

"Ten thousand dollars would have been a lot for someone who wanted to get their business back—Biga, *no!*" I tugged on the leash as Biga headed for what looked like a pile of cat poop.

The mayor laughed, the first sign of humor I'd seen from her in weeks. "They do say it tastes like candy to dogs."

"It's disgusting! I love my dog, but there are limits." I pulled Biga back and gave him a liver treat instead, which satisfied him.

The mayor stood up and leaned against the stair railing.

"Corinne, you said you had some news."

The mayor rubbed her eyes and looked over at me blearily.

"I had a talk with Gordon Dabney, our Chamber of Commerce president. He said Barb's old space in Boulder Creek has been leased. And--it was leased for the same price Barb paid."

"What?" This just sounded wrong. "Did he say who the new tenant is?"

"Gordon didn't know. I tried to get hold of the building's new owner—Carlton-Foreman Associates. I've left two messages and haven't heard back."

The mayor sighed and looked out over the not-so-photogenic backside of the businesses on the next street over—dumpsters, old crates, piles of old lumber and weeds.

"What I want to do is drive over to Boulder Creek and see the space myself. Try to meet with the new owner." She looked over at me. "Want to team up on this, Gracie? There's no denying you're better at this than I am."

Coming from the mayor, this was a high compliment. I was shocked I was hearing it. But this week would not work for me. Not only was I scrambling to find the access codes, I had a busy bakery to manage.

"I wish I could. I can't leave the bakery this week."

The mayor frowned then she looked at me questioningly. "I get that. There's something off about this situation. If they were so determined to raise the rent, why would they keep it the same for a new tenant? I want to get justice for Barb. You okay with me checking in with you, to talk through what I find out?"

"Yes. Please do."

The mayor could be difficult to deal with sometimes, but her motives were good. Maeve had said it best a few months ago: "Mayor C has a heart of gold, but she wants to make sure nobody finds out about it."

It felt odd not to be investigating. Barb's death was an intriguing puzzle, and it would have been a great distraction to keep me from worrying about Friday's meeting with the dissidents.

I just couldn't do it this time.

After loading Biga in the car and waving goodbye to Brad in the squad car, I headed home to get ready for my outing with Elana at The Riverside.

My dad was dressed in slacks and a shirt with a bow tie, ready for Mary Jo to start making dinner with him and play a board game. Mary Jo didn't seem like a board game person, but she'd cheerfully agreed to it. I envisioned them leaning over the table playing *Chutes and Ladders*. But I knew it was probably some nerdy game given to him by one of his students.

"Hey," I said, as I came in lugging Biga's crate. I let him out and he headed straight for my dad. "Does Mary Jo dress up to cook dinner, too?"

My dad smirked as he straightened his bowtie. "I have my standards, and I like to maintain them."

"Elana's picking me up to go to The Riverside a little before 7. We'll come back here for a bit when she drops me off, but I won't be out long."

My dad smiled mysteriously. "I believe I saw the local operative outside today. In a black car with those darkened windows."

"Was it Brad?" I asked, half serious, half joking.

"Someone was in the driver's seat, but I couldn't see much. Good to know they're here."

Soon Mary Jo was at the door, carrying a bag that smelled amazing—garlic and some kind of hearty tomato sauce that smelled homemade.

I hugged Mary Jo warmly. "Hope you two have fun tonight. Will there will be leftovers?"

Mary Jo smiled and gave me a kiss on the cheek.

"I'll set aside some for you, Gracie, don't you worry."

Mary Jo and I had come a long way in the past year. It had taken me a while to warm up to her. As I got to know her, I realized the fact that she was very different than my mother was a good thing. Besides, she and my mom had both recognized that underneath my dad's reserve and social stumbling was a kind, warmhearted man.

Elana came by right before 7 and tapped on the door. I saw her through the peephole, dressed in her sparkly pink jacket.

If there was a band playing tonight, I knew she was going to make me get up and dance. Maybe I'd gotten better at it. It was more likely that I'd learned not to care how goofy I looked doing it.

"It's been so long since we've done this," Elana said after we'd buckled up in her Audi and she was backing out of our driveway. It was as if she'd been saving up all her words for me and they all came gushing out.

"What has it been—three months, Gracie? We *so* need to catch up. Did I tell you we've decided to get a cat instead of a dog? Kirk thought we should start small, and a cat would be lower maintenance. They seem unfriendly to me, though. I think cats are narcissists." Once we got on the highway, she blurted out. "So, tell me what's going on?"

I swallowed and thought about how I'd say this. I didn't want to give her too much "juicy goss" as she called it. I'd keep it low key. I could talk about Barb's case.

"Mayor C came up with something about Barb D'Amato's case today," I said as Elana pulled onto the highway. "The new owner of Barb's building just leased her old spot to a new tenant for the exact same rate Barb *used* to pay."

"What the hell? So the big increase was just for Barb?" Elana frowned, keeping her eyes on the road. "She had to close down her business because of that. Maybe the new owner just didn't like Barb."

"Could be," I said. Mayor C had sounded more excited about this development than Elana was sounding right now. "Still it's odd, don't you think?"

"Are you going to investigate?"

"With the bakery, I don't have time. Mayor C's going to look into it."

Elana shot a quick look over at me as we drove down the highway.

"Hey, you didn't tell me what you wanted to brainstorm about. It wasn't about Barb's death, was it?"

"No. It's about my ex-husband." I saw her raise her eyebrows as she drove. "He had some very important information—which I need to get my hands on. He did this to me before. He hid something really important in Biga's feeding ball, just to spite me. And now, I think he's done it again. I looked through my computer and anything else of mine he could have had access to, but I couldn't find it. I looked through baking stuff, cookbooks, and equipment that I had in our house in Seattle. Nothing."

As the sun set and the temperatures dropped, Elana steered us down the road toward the bright lights of The Riverside.

"Let me think about this. From what I know about Ben," she said. "I mean, I know *some* about him. He's super smart, selfish, and good-looking. Remember you showed me that picture of him in the Italian suit?"

"Yes, I remember." I said with a heavy sigh. Now I wished I hadn't shown Elana the photo. "I'd say those things are all true."

Elana was quiet as we pulled into The Riverside parking lot.

"Now to figure out where Ben would have hidden something. But I can't think about this till I've had an appetizer." She parked the car in a spot near the front door. "Let's talk inside."

We walked through the double doors into the saloon's large, wood-paneled main room and took a table near the bar.

Being here with Elana, with the threat that someone else was hunting me down, brought back bad memories. I shivered as I thought of the Russian spies who'd stalked me last fall. As we walked to our table, I scanned the room for anyone with Volkov's tall, thin frame and dark hair. Or Zofia Zbirak's big pouty lips.

As usual, Elana and I were only interested in drinks and appetizers. Since it was a Wednesday night, there was only a small band playing, probably local musicians. A willowy woman with warm brown skin sang a ballad, jazz style, while a keyboard player and bassist accompanied her. A drummer played a light background rhythm with brushes on a drum kit.

It was soft and soothing to my tired brain. I was sure I wouldn't be on the dance floor tonight. And I was glad about that.

"So this info you're looking for," Elana took a sip of the cosmo our waiter just set in front of her. "Are you saying it would be digital? Like on a storage device—a USB stick or something like that?"

"Yes, I think so. Almost all of Ben's life was spent on devices. They were his world. His language."

The waiter delivered our chips and guacamole and a plate of fried calamari. He also set in front of us a new treat from the menu, courtesy of Reggie—small bao buns stuffed with chicken in peanut satay sauce. We both dug in. After a busy day, I was ravenous.

"I'm thinking of what would be on Ben's mind when you left him. Which you did, right?"

I nodded. I hadn't wanted to go into the details of the witness protection/FBI story with Elana. I didn't tell her I'd turned him in. Or that he was now in a maximum-security prison.

"What would he miss most about you?" She watched me as she took another sip of her cosmo.

"Hmmm. Well, this sounds weird but it's true," I said with a shrug. "Probably my looks."

"Of course. Your body." Elana said suddenly, her eyes wide with understanding. "You're a good-looking woman, Gracie, and this guy hangs around computer geeks all day. You're gorgeous. I'm sure he misses that. So what dress or outfit did he love to see you in?"

This was a strange twist in the conversation. I turned red as I thought about it. But Elana might have a point.

"I have an orange mini dress that looked great on me. I felt amazing when I wore it. Oh, and a little black dress, I guess. I haven't had an opportunity to wear it here in River Grove. It's home in my closet." I ate another chip loaded with Reggie's own guacamole. "He really liked it. He'd ask me to wear it when we went out."

"We need to look at those dresses, Gracie," Elana said with a serious look on her face.

This was a strange idea. But I did my brainstorming with Elana for one reason: she thought of things I didn't.

After we talked about everything else happening in our lives and were scraping the last of the guac from the bowl, Elana drove us back to my house. As we entered the door, I saw

Mary Jo leaning against my dad's shoulder on the sofa. Both were fast asleep. A board game was spread out on the coffee table, with cards and game pieces set up. The pieces looked like they hadn't been moved from their starting position.

"Look at those two. They're adorable," Elana whispered to me as we headed down the hall to my room, Biga following us.

"Looks like they didn't even start," I said, with a quiet chuckle. "So much for game night."

I slid open my closet. I pulled the hangers with my dresses toward us and started sorting through them.

"This was *my* favorite." I pulled the orange dress out. It was sleeveless, short and swingy, and the color brought out the warm tones in my auburn hair. "And it's got *pockets*."

"Oooh, I like this one. Not everybody looks good in orange, but this would be perfect for you."

I laid it on the bed and thrust my hand into a pocket. Nothing but a bit of lint. In the other pocket, I found a receipt from a pub in Seattle.

"I need an excuse to wear this again." I held it up to myself. There's something about a piece of clothing that makes you feel terrific when you wear it. The memory came back to me, that feeling of confidence, and it made me want to figure out where to wear it again.

We pawed through the rest of the items on hangers until I got to the black dress. It was cute and showed off my curves. I held it up to myself and remembered how Ben had looked at me when I wore it—then immediately tried to forget that look.

"Damn, that's a great dress," Elana said with envy in her voice. I laid it out on the bed and we patted it down.

"I feel something in there," Elana said as she felt the sash. "How do you get it out? I don't see a zipper or snap."

The dress had a sash with a velcro closing. When we went out, it was handy for stashing an ID and some cash.

I felt for the Velcro and pulled the sides of the opening apart.

And there I saw it.

A relic from an ancient civilization.

A small, blue, 3-1/4-inch floppy disk.

Chapter Twenty-Five

"What is *this*?"

Elana stared at the flat, square plastic object with a rectangular metal covering at the top. She picked it up. "I remember now. Kirk and I saw one of these at the Computer History Museum over in Sunnyvale."

My dad had used these with his old IBM desktop computer. A few years before I was born.

My first thought was, we wouldn't be able to find a computer that would let us access the contents of this disk. Even if it did contain the pipeline access codes.

"It's a floppy disk," I said, turning it over in my hand. What an ass Ben was, putting the information on an old storage device like this. Again, Ben had done whatever he could to make my life difficult.

"It's not even floppy. Why would they call it that?" Elana laughed. "I bet Kirk could find something old at Blue-Surf that could run this. Let me take it home with me."

I had less than 48 hours. I tried not to panic. Or to look like I was panicking.

"That's okay, El. I think I can figure out how to get what I need from this. But your investigator hunch was on point, my friend."

"Glad to help. And we totally needed a night out."

"We did." I hugged her. "And you'll always be my brainstormer-in-chief."

I'd call Maura and Jeremy as soon as Elana left. They worked for the government, so I wouldn't be surprised to hear that somewhere *somebody* had an ancient desktop computer that was still in use.

I went to my room, with Biga following close behind. The sleeping people in the living room were not at all interesting to him. I flopped down on my bed and called on the burner phone.

At first Maura was ecstatic—as much as that was possible with Maura—when I called to tell her I might have found the codes. Then I explained how I'd found them and what format they were in.

"On a floppy disk," Maura repeated in disbelief. "Like one of those from the 1980s?"

"I thought if anyone could figure out how to read the info on the disk, it would be you guys. Do you have access to a very old computer?"

"Hawk will be by in a few minutes to pick up the disk. We'll put our computer forensics unit to work on it and see what we can find, Gracie." She paused. "I still can't believe you found it in an old dress."

Once the agents figured out if the disk contained the codes, we'd talk about a plan for Friday's meeting with SABRE.

I had no idea what to expect. The dissidents were obviously angry at Ben for taking their money and not giving them the goods. I was the only target they had for their anger.

After I set the burner phone down, I didn't have the energy to get up and change my clothes. I heard movement in the living room, where it sounded like my dad and Mary Jo had woken up. I heard yawns and muffled laughter. I heard the door open, and Mary Jo had left.

The water was running in my dad's bathroom, as he brushed his teeth.

A few minutes later, my phone lit up with a text from Hawk.

> I'm outside. Let me know you got this, and I'll come to the door for the disk.

After a quick handoff to Hawk, I locked the door and went back to bed, still in my clothes.

With Biga was cuddled up next to me, my exhaustion won out over my anxiety.

Before I knew it, I was out.

Chapter Twenty-Six

I got out of bed at 4 a.m., groggy after a night of weird dreams.

In one, Volkov and Zbirak pursued me on Highway 1 along the coast—on scooters capable of speeds of 70 mph.

It was Thursday. One day until I was expected to hand over the codes, if they even existed on the floppy disk.

I was trusting that the agents would come up with a plan so that the group didn't actually use the codes to bring down a pipeline, even though they were sure that would help their cause.

I cautiously padded down the hall and saw the game board still set up in our living room. I yawned as I went into the kitchen, dumping twice as much coffee into the coffeemaker as I usually did. Then I took a shower, dug up clothes to change into, and ate the leftover chicken satay bao buns I'd brought home from The Riverside last night. I wondered why it was that leftovers were way more delicious than regular breakfast food.

I slipped the burner phone into my purse. I'd need to keep in touch with the agents. I wanted to hear if the computer forensics lab was able to find the codes on the disk or whether my searches had been a waste of time.

The RGPD squad car was parked in the alley, next to the back steps. This time, the chief's voice came across the car's loudspeaker.

"Good morning, Gracie."

I laughed and saw him wave. The guy had given up a lot of his time to keep watch over us.

Beck came in an hour later, with eggs from her chickens to use for our new, larger batches of brioche. She started loading them into the egg compartment of the industrial fridge. I kept tab of her contributions, and I did give her compensation in her paycheck. The eggs were way better than anything we could buy at the store.

"Hey, Beck. Can you make an egg on toast for the chief? The guy's been keeping an eye on the alley for the past two days. I want to make sure he's happy with his comfort food. I'll make him his drip coffee."

Beck smiled. "I'll get going on it before I start anything else."

I made a pot of drip in the industrial coffeemaker, as Beck heated up the grill and began making the buttered toast and over-medium egg.

In a few minutes I went down the back steps to deliver his coffee and breakfast. The sun hadn't risen yet. The chief had a light attached to his dashboard and was reading through paperwork. For the past two days, he'd turned the car into his office.

I tapped on the window. The chief rolled it down and his face brightened as he saw what I was carrying.

"Aww, Gracie." He eagerly took the plate with the egg on toast and then grabbed the coffee to put in his cupholder.

I handed him a fork. "You didn't have to do this, chief."

"It's my job. I am managing to get some work done while I'm out here. Less interruptions." He took a big gulp of his coffee, then sighed with happiness. "I know everyone thinks it's because of Barb, but the fact is, we're still not sure who killed her. It's not a bad thing to patrol the alley."

This was my entrée to ask him a favor.

"Can I get in the passenger side? I have a question for you."

The chief shrugged. "Sure, Gracie. Let's talk." He unlocked the door for me.

I slid into the seat. "Did you talk to Corinne last night?"

"She did say she wanted to talk to me, but I've been a little busy the past twenty-four hours."

I wondered if the agents had enlisted him to do more for them.

"The mayor talked to Chamber of Commerce president Dabney about Barb's case. And he said the space for Barb's shop in Boulder Creek has been leased for the same amount Barb paid for ten years."

"Somebody got a deal, huh? Who's the tenant?"

"Mayor C's trying to find out."

I turned to him. "I want to ask you a favor. I don't have the authority. Can you get a copy of the cashier's check Barb cashed at Boulder Creek Credit Union? To find out who ordered the check?"

The chief studied my face and turned to think about this.

"I think I can do that. Let me get the process going."

I made the chief promise to text me if he needed more

coffee—or lunch. Then I went back inside to prepare for what was surely going to be another busy day.

Maeve and Rose came in and got to work with their prep.

I put on a familiar, upbeat pop playlist, mostly because I needed some energizing music to keep my mood up. My coworkers knew the words by now and started singing along.

"Mayor C said she saw you at The Riverside last night with your friend Elana," Maeve said with a mischievous look. "Glad to see you got a girls' night for yourself this week."

"No hangover for *me*, though." I shot back at her, remembering my staff's late night drinking session at The Riverside the night before.

Rose and Beck both went *oooooooh* and looked between the two of us, trying not to laugh at our smackdown.

"That is fair," Maeve said calmly, the corners of her mouth turning up. "But then, you are *older* and wiser, Gracie."

I smirked. "It wasn't like I never had a night like that ten years ago." Then I made a bold statement, considering my fears about tomorrow's deadline with SABRE. "Sometime soon let's plan a back-room girls' night out. In a week or two, when things aren't so crazy."

"Let's do it!" Maeve called out, followed by enthusiastic *yesses* from Beck and Rose.

Once we opened our door, it was another nonstop flood of customers—especially at lunch. Some River Grovians were just coming in for the first time to try lunch at our renovated bakery. Others were out-of-towners who'd read about the expanded offerings. Our location made it easy to drop by on the way to somewhere fun. It was summer and the Santa Cruz Mountains were filled with people wanting to hike the trails, ride the Roaring Camp Railroad to see the redwoods up close, and drive out to the coast and the Santa Cruz Beach Boardwalk amusement park.

Elise and Daisy were getting their routine down and, despite the crowd, the line for lunch went fast.

Maeve had baked a double order of flatbread for wraps, so customers left with what they'd wanted.

At 1 p.m., while the lunch crowd was still filling the dining area, I took a break to get Biga outside for a walk. I kept the burner phone with me, in case the agents called with updates on the contents of the disk.

I texted Hawk to tell him I was walking with Biga over to the greenspace in front of The Riverside Saloon. It should be safe. We'd be out in the open, in a place where lots of people gathered during the day in the summer.

Biga's short little legs worked overtime as he made his way down the sidewalk. As we passed Speed Spot Motors, Jeanne Daniels saw us from the window and came out to see Biga. He was thrilled to get the love and when she bent down to pet him, he immediately slathered her hands with sloppy kisses.

When we got to the greenspace, Biga tugged on the leash. He'd spotted some bushes by the redwoods. Since that was why we were here, I let him take the lead and waited patiently while he sniffed at and watered almost every one.

Walking around the greenspace made me feel nostalgic for the popup. When we'd worked out here every day, I couldn't wait until we were back in the bakery. I sat down on a bench at the edge of the greenspace, leaned back and stretched my legs out.

Biga lay on the grass in the sun by my feet and closed his eyes.

I dozed off a bit but woke immediately when Biga began growling. I looked up to see a dark shadow on the grass in front of me. My heart pounded.

I turned around cautiously to see the gaunt, bearded face of Henryk Volkov.

Chapter Twenty-Seven

Mrs. *Morrison*."

I made no sudden moves, and slowly looked behind me at the man, sure he was holding a gun on me.

He wasn't. He held an iPhone in his hands and was wearing tight black jeans, a turtleneck and a black jacket. Not the best thing to be wearing in today's sunny, 87-degree weather.

"That's not my name, Henryk. I'm Gracie Markley, and I did not sell you the access codes to the pipeline. My ex-husband lied to you when he said we were working together. I'm sorry he didn't give you what you paid for, but I wasn't involved in the sale in any way. We are now divorced."

Volkov let out a deep, hoarse laugh. Biga growled.

"Ah, very nice, Mrs. Morrison. I know you are lying. His friend Mr. Kyle Burnett told us of the little enterprise you started together. Two lovebirds working side-by-side to sell the world's most valuable secrets to the highest bidders. I'm sure it's a very profitable business."

His words made me want to throw up.

"This is not true." Sweat trickled uncomfortably down my back. "My ex-husband is now in a maximum-security prison in Florence, Colorado. I haven't seen or talked to him in almost three years."

"Oh, we know where he is, Mrs. Morrison. But your husband and Mr. Burnett assured SABRE that the pipeline access codes were in a safe place with you. You will give these to us tomorrow. We have grown tired of waiting. The Satrovanian people have waited centuries to be free. Our time has come."

"What happens if I don't have the codes?" I asked in a shaky voice.

Volkov reached into the chest pocket of his jacket and slowly drew out a shiny black handgun.

"We have many ways to get them out of you, Mrs. Morrison." He held the gun there to prove his point, then slid it back into his jacket. "We're a desperate and angry people, and we will use them to get what we want. We will see you tomorrow at noon. Shark Fin Cove."

Biga didn't like how Volkov was talking to me. His growling escalated into a bark. I reached down to pick him up and held him close against my chest to keep him quiet.

Footsteps crunched on dry pine needles behind me. I looked around to see Volkov was gone. Not behind the bench, not on the street. Not as far as I could see, in the grove of redwoods at the other end of the space.

I quickly texted Hawk, then copied my text and sent it to the chief.

> Just saw Volkov at the greenspace by The Riverside. He has a gun. He threatened me for the codes.

Hawk texted me back:

> We're on it. Are you safe now? Can you get back?

I texted yes.

The chief offered to come get me. I told him I'd walk back with Biga myself. There would be people on the street around me on the way, and I didn't think I'd be in danger.

Apparently, word among the agents traveled as fast as the gossip in River Grove.

Three minutes later, I got a call from Maura.

Her voice was firm, and she sounded concerned.

"Are you okay, Gracie? Did he hurt you?"

I stood up, my knees wobbling, as what I'd just experienced hit me.

"He had a gun, but he didn't use it. I'm fine."

"Gracie, we read the disk and copied all the information. We've got the pipeline access codes and a full list of the system's vulnerabilities. Ben stumbled upon some very detailed and dangerous information. It's more than we thought he had. If SABRE gets this, they'll bring down the pipeline and much of the Balkans with it."

"I read about SABRE's mission. It sounds like their government treats their people terribly. They just want rights for all, and that's something they've never had."

"There are better ways to get that than giving them the codes Ben sold them," Maura said. "We've been formulating a plan for tomorrow, and we want to talk to you about it at your place tonight. Jeremy and I will be there at 6 p.m."

I didn't want to admit it to Maura, but I was scared. I didn't want to deal with this. I wanted to bake bread and sing songs with my staff in the back room. I wanted to figure out who killed Barb D'Amato. The thought still nagged me: Did her death have anything to do with SABRE?

Ben had put me in a horrible situation, and there was no way to get through this other than to trust in the agents' plan.

I just hoped it was a good one.

BACK AT THE BAKERY, after setting Biga back in his pen, I washed up at the big sink and got back to work.

"Are you okay, Gracie?" Maeve glanced at me as she passed by to take a tray of warm flatbread up to the lunch counter. "You're looking quite pale."

"I'm fine. I need to eat something soon." I was very hungry, but my stomach was still queasy from my meetup with Volkov.

"Want me to ask Elise and Daisy to make you a wrap?"

"A small one would be nice," I said, as I headed to check the sourdough loaves in the proofer. "Just chicken and vegetables."

"You got it, boss." Maeve went up to the counter.

I couldn't spare any more time to go talk to the chief. I put my apron back on and slid my personal phone into the front pocket. As soon as I did, it buzzed.

The chief's text.

Gracie, you ok?

Back at bakery.

Good. Now stay put.

I bristled a little bit at the command, but I knew he

meant well. He was worried about my safety and had done everything he could to ensure it this week.

As the day went on, the tenseness in my gut and the shakiness in my legs went away. I threw myself into my duties. Rose and I sliced brioche loaves for the lunch counter, and she excitedly told me about the fantasy books she'd been reading. She'd just started an Ursula K. LeGuin novel after finishing the *Lord of the Rings* trilogy. She loved the character of Samwise Gamgee, because, as she said, he was "the real hero of the story, without actually being the hero."

It made me want to read more outside my usual genre of murder mysteries—a choice, which lately, had been feeling a little too on the nose for my life.

At 2:30, we closed after ushering the last customers from the dining area. With the heat outside, everyone wanted to stay inside in the air-conditioned dining area. I didn't blame them. The back of my t-shirt was damp from sweat.

I was scared of tomorrow's meetup at Shark Fin Cove, but if nothing terrifying happened with SABRE, at least it would be cooler than River Grove.

When I got a chance, I texted Nate.

Late dinner tonight? I miss you.

Me, too. My place this time?

I need a change of scenery! 7:15?

Perfect. 🩶

I took Biga home and showered, just to get the sweat off me. My dad and I split an ale that had been chilling in the fridge. It wasn't the warm British pub style, which my dad was used to but I couldn't stomach. Gulping down the fresh, ice-cold ale helped on a hot, sweaty evening as we waited for Maura and Jeremy.

I told my dad about Volkov and what he had said about Kyle assuring him that Ben and I were a tech spy team.

My dad shook his head. The lines on his face looked deeper tonight. "Gracie. I should have said something about Ben years ago."

"I wouldn't have listened." I sighed and leaned back on the couch, pressing the cold beer glass to my forehead. "I thought Ben was amazing. So smart with such a bright future. I thought I was lucky to have him."

"You deserved better," he said, and in the light it looked like his eyes were misting.

I smiled and thought of seeing Nate in a little over an hour. I thought of the bakery, with my growing staff, which I'd decided to call the Back Room Girls. I really had to make t-shirts for us.

And Beck, the first one I hired. The one I took a big chance on. I was both looking forward to working with her at the bakery for a long, long time—and hoping she had the chance to become a mother, something I knew she wanted very much.

"I have more than I could ever have imagined." I took a sip of ale. "I hope I get to enjoy it a little while longer. Like past tomorrow."

A few seconds later, the doorbell rang. My father looked through the peephole and then let Maura and Jeremy in. As they stepped in, Maura looked behind her, up and down the street, then shut and locked the door behind her.

"Let's go into the study," Maura said, and we moved

into my dad's office, taking our seats in the small room. As usual, we were almost knocking our knees together.

"A lot has happened today," Jeremy said, meeting my eyes. "Gracie, I'm sorry Volkov threatened you at the green-space. He and SABRE are desperate—and they are set on their plan to use the codes to shut down the oil pipeline and hold the entire country of Satrovania hostage. We were surprised at how much information was on that disk."

"Our sources in the country tell us that the information is still up to date. And the Satrovanian government would be completely caught off guard by the shutdown," Maura said. "With the codes and system vulnerabilities, SABRE could do a lot of harm. Not just to Satrovania, but to other countries in the region also dependent on the oil. We can't afford to destabilize the region for this."

"So what do you propose to do?" My dad looked at the two agents. "Is Gracie supposed to hand the codes over to these people? They've threatened to do serious harm to her if she doesn't bring them."

Maura nodded. "We understand that, John. We are preparing to stake out the area around the cove early tomorrow. We've lined up help from law enforcement agencies and our local operative. Our plan is for Gracie to hand over altered codes—so they look like the real thing, but they do not work."

"But Volkov thinks this is the only way to bargain for change in his country," I said. I wasn't impressed by Volkov's social skills or gun waving, but I had sympathy for his cause. "I've read about the monarchy there. People who aren't of a certain ethnicity and social status don't have the same rights. It's been that way for centuries. These people are desperate to get attention for their cause."

"If they shut down the pipeline, it won't bring the

changes they want," Jeremy said, looking a little sympathetic himself. "I understand your concerns, Gracie. We're not experts in international diplomacy and that's not our job. Our job is to keep you safe. And to minimize the damage from what Ben set up."

The agents launched into the details of their plan. Maura would meet me at the bakery at 11 to get me set up with the wire, so the agents and local operative could hear our conversation.

I would drive up to the cove by myself and park at the meeting place, then hike down to the beach by the large shark fin rock formation. Maura and Jeremy would arrive at the cove's parking lot early, disguised as friends taking a picnic down to the beach. The local operative, who would be armed, would sneak back, as if heading back to the parking lot, then hide behind a niche in the cliff near the meeting place.

"You will have the codes and vulnerability list in printed form, then also give them a USB stick with a digital copy," Jeremy continued. "That's what they asked for from Ben. We want this to go smoothly, Gracie, so if Volkov starts talking about Ben and you working together, don't get triggered. Do not correct him. Your job is to get this to them as promised."

I took in my breath. "Okay. So there's no way they're going to know you've altered the codes?"

"The only people who'd spot that would be the technicians who will go into the system to activate the codes. As far as we know, the people who would do this are back in Satrovania."

As far as we know wasn't very reassuring.

"Any other questions? Are we good?" Maura turned to me, then my dad.

My dad shook his head. But I knew from the hollow look in his eyes. He was scared for me.

"I will see you at 11 a.m. in the alley, Gracie. With the codes." Maura stood up and gathered her purse. She looked across at my dad. "And, John, Hawk will be here in front of your house in the truck tomorrow."

Jeremy picked up his briefcase.

"Gracie, we're confident you can do this. After all the things you've come through over the past two years, I can't think of anyone more capable." He smiled encouragingly. "You've got this."

After the agents left the house, I gulped down the rest of my ale. Then I took Biga out for a runaround in the backyard, while I thought long and hard about the life choices that had led me to this place.

Nate had made salmon and broccolini, two of my favorite things. Along with French butter and a warmed-up loaf of sourdough from The Laughing Loaf, also two of my favorite things.

He'd set the small table in his kitchen with a white tablecloth and tapers in vintage candle holders. It looked simple but posh. For some reason, I thought of the last meal prisoners on death row get, before execution.

I hugged him and even though this meal was waiting for me, I didn't let go of him for a while.

"This is perfect."

"You met with the agents tonight," he asked as we sat down. "How did it go?"

"It was...okay, I guess. But I should tell you that I saw Volkov at the greenspace earlier when I was walking Biga. It was intense." I didn't tell Nate that he'd threatened me with a gun. "He's betting everything on shutting down the pipeline. That it will force the king's hand and get their cause noticed."

Then I told him about the agents' plan for the meetup at Shark Fin Cove. He frowned as I talked about what I'd be doing tomorrow, and about the altered codes we'd be giving to Volkov and SABRE.

"The local contact will be close by, along with the agents. I'll be wired, so they'll hear our conversation as I hand over the information."

As I talked, Nate turned pale and the muscles in his face tightened. "The agents are using you, Gracie. If they'd gotten hold of the actual codes and shut down the pipeline, this could be an international incident. If the Satrovanians realize they're not getting the real codes, what happens to you?"

"They'll have law enforcement in place—"

"Gracie, the letter they left at the bakery said they didn't want law enforcement there. What happens if they find out you're wired—or that the agents are there?" Lines deepened across his forehead. "It's not right that you have to deal with this. You did nothing to make this situation happen. You're having to deal with what Ben left you with. And what the King of Satrovania left his people. It's not your problem to fix."

And through our conversation, I saw anger simmering and bubbling to the surface, as he saw someone he cared about being treated unjustly. When his brother Nico had been killed behind the Laughing Loaf, Nate's anger had come out. Now his anger was directed at the agents for putting me in this dangerous position.

"That's it." He looked across the table at me. I saw fury in his face, along with a new look I didn't recognize. Resolve, maybe. "I'll be there at Shark Fin Cove tomorrow."

Chapter Twenty-Eight

I slept horribly that night.

Biga got so annoyed by my tossing, he finally jumped off the bed to seek a more peaceful place to sleep.

As I lay in bed, staring at the ceiling, I thought it through. How would I deal with my absence at the bakery? Chances are it would be as busy as Monday. Many people had Fridays off or worked from home in River Grove. They might come to the bakery today for coffee, to work on their laptops in the dining area, or to pick up lunch.

How could I leave my staff with this?

I'd have to be gone for at least two hours, assuming things went okay with the pipeline code transfer. I'd put off telling Beck and the staff. I was hoping, unrealistically, that the situation with the codes would be resolved—or that the agents would come up with a solution that did not involve me.

I hated to lie to my staff. Especially Beck. I couldn't look into her big, innocent eyes and tell her I had to take two hours off to go to a doctor's appointment. Or that I had to deal with a crime-related matter—like Barb's murder.

I certainly couldn't do that on one of our busiest weeks ever.

I sat up in bed and reached for the second book of the *Lord of the Rings* trilogy. When Rose and I had talked about books, she said she'd loved the series and especially the quote from Sam Gamgee, Frodo's loyal friend and companion. Sam encourages Frodo by telling him that the great stories of old are full of darkness and danger. You think, how could things ever be bright and happy again? But in the end, even darkness must pass.

This meetup with SABRE would pass. Today would pass. I would in some way survive it.

At least I hoped.

Finally, at 3 a.m., I got out of bed, showered, and dressed. I brewed another double batch of pre-coffee to tide me over till I got to the bakery.

Biga was in with my dad, so I couldn't say goodbye. He'd stay home today.

I got there a half hour before the chief showed up in the alley at 4:30 a.m. As usual when I was scared, I turned on every light in the place. I didn't feel like turning on the music.

My phone buzzed in my apron pocket. The chief texted me, surprised to see the lights on in the bakery.

You okay in there?

Fine. Couldn't sleep. Came in to do some work.

Hang in there, Gracie.

thx chief

I tried to prep everything I could, to help my staff when I was out during our busy lunch hour. I made sure the fridge was full of enough sliced meats and cheeses, cut veggies, and condiments. Maeve would bake the breads and the double batch of flatbread this morning and have it ready for lunch service. She knew what to do. We should be fine.

I mixed up and laminated three batches of scones, sliced them into wedges, and wrapped them to go in the freezer for quick baking if needed. Then I dipped into the sourdough starter for a generous amount of discard and mixed up sourdough starter chocolate chip cookies. Because, if everything else sold out, there would be cookies on hand, and who's going to complain about having to order cookies?

I felt like I'd been there for hours by the time Beck came in, cheerful. "'Morning, Gracie!"

"Good morning." I looked in her direction as I mixed cookie dough. I must have looked worried because she immediately stopped at the fridge and looked at me before putting on her apron.

"Is everything okay?"

"I need to leave for about two hours today, from 11 till about 1." I took a deep breath, but I couldn't quite keep my lips from trembling. "I'm sorry. I can't tell you what it is, and I don't want to make something up. I know it's going to be crazy here today, and I am sorry to ditch you all."

Beck's face showed only understanding. "If it's important, then you have to go. You don't need to tell me why. Don't worry." She smiled encouragingly. "We can handle it. If this was Monday, maybe not. But every day we've gotten a little better at this."

I remembered Reggie McFerrin's hippie wisdom from a few days ago.

The bakery isn't just you—it's a community. It's not dependent on you, Gracie. Release it.

Maybe if I left for a couple of hours, even on this busy day of opening week, it would be okay.

Then again, maybe that was the least of my worries.

I hugged Beck.

"Be careful, Gracie." She put her hands on my shoulders and looked at me, as if she'd get some clue as to what I was going off to. "I will be saying a little prayer for you."

"Um, sure." I mumbled awkwardly. "Thank you, Beck."

At 11 a.m., as the lunch team set up sandwich and wrap fixings at the front counter, I hung my apron up. Maeve was slicing bread and Rose was heading to the front to work the counter. I grabbed my purse with both my phones in it and nodded to Beck. Then I quietly slipped out the back door.

I didn't see the squad car in the alley. Maybe the chief had gone ahead to the meetup. I hoped he wasn't going to drive down to Shark Fin Cove in the squad car loudly announcing his presence as law enforcement.

Maura stood next to my car, her hair in a ponytail. She handed me the small tote bag in her hand.

"Gracie, here are the codes—the USB and the printout. I've got the wire. Let's put this thing on."

We sat in my car, and when I lowered my shirt, she deftly clipped the tiny microphone to my bra strap. "There you go."

"Wait, that's it?" I thought there would be more involved, a big battery pack and some cord dangling down under my shirt.

Then Maura pulled something familiar from her beach bag. "I almost forgot. We need to put the tracker back on your car. We want SABRE to see you coming, so they don't panic."

She got out of the car and bent down to attach the tracker to the bumper. She came back, opened the passenger side door, and peered in at me.

"That's it. I need to go now. I have to pick Jeremy and a puppy up in Davenport nearby on the coast. I'll see you at the cove. Just remember. When you see us, you don't know us."

Sure, whatever. I sighed.

I got on Highway 9, which was slower than usual, since everyone wanted to take the less trafficked road to the beach on a beautiful day. It was sunny, and it was heating up. Still, I felt the temperatures ease as I neared Highway 1 on the coast. I went north, heading toward the small town of Davenport.

I'd just turned onto 1 North, when my phone rang. I pressed to answer the call through my audio system.

"Gracie, the chief here. I'm in Boulder Creek at the credit union with Mayor C. We have a copy of the check. Barb's check was issued through an international bank in Satrovania. Her name isn't on it, but it's from the account of Zofia Zbirak."

I shuddered. Everything was coming together, just as I went to wrap things up with SABRE. My suspicions were being confirmed: Barb received a payout for identifying me. And then, she was killed to cover up SABRE's trail.

They could do the same to me after I gave them the pipeline codes.

"Was there any explanation with the check? Like a reason for payment?"

"It just says for 'valuable services'," the Chief said. "We interviewed Amora Davis, too. Asked her if Barb told her why she'd received such a big check. Amora said when she asked about it, Barb changed the subject."

"The SABRE group paid her. Probably to confirm my identity."

I still wasn't sure exactly how much the chief knew about my situation in WITSEC or my background. We always stopped short of it in our conversations, as if we both knew we weren't supposed to talk about it.

"We don't know that was the reason." Then I heard the Chief talking with someone else in the background. "Listen, Gracie, I've got to go. There's a couple of leads we need to follow up in Barb's case. Corinne found out who the new tenant is. It's kind of a surprise, but what isn't these days?"

I hung up and continued north on the highway. Shark Fin Cove was about three-quarters of a mile south of the town of Davenport. Soon I saw the unmarked Shark Fin Cove parking lot.

I quickly pulled off the highway and veered into the dirt lot, my heart pounding. There were three cars parked, two of them small SUVs. Neither looked familiar, but then I saw a couple get out of the Honda, dressed in light windbreakers, shorts and goofy-looking sunhats. They were laughing and trying to manage a small dog on a leash. I realized, startled, that this was Maura and Jeremy. Still looking completely engaged with each other's company, they headed down the trail to the beach, as if they were being dragged by their energetic puppy.

Then at the far end of the small lot, I saw it.

The blue Chevy Malibu. Volkov and Zbirak's car.

I spotted the trailhead for the path leading down to the beach and the shark fin rock configuration jutting up out of the water, hard to miss.

I looked down into the tote bag to see the USB stick and

the printout of the codes, bound in a report folder. I felt like I was about to hand in my semester final project for a college class, after staying up all night to finish it.

Tote bag in hand, I got out of my car and started in on the trail, which led down to the spot Volkov had marked on the map. I focused on the rough beauty of the surroundings, a place of sheer cliffs and a secluded beach. The air smelled differently here than down in Santa Cruz, which tended to carry the scents of corn dogs and fried food. The smell here was sharp, salty, and tinged with the smell of dead things.

I followed the trail as it descended sharply to the shore. The path was rough, and I tried to step carefully and deliberately around loose rocks and dirt.

As I neared the sand, I saw a bike wedged into a nook in the rock. I knew exactly who that bike belonged to.

Nate had done what he'd said he would do.

Looming before me was the large fin rock formation in the middle of the churning, teal-green water. I walked left, per the instructions, till I saw people standing on the other side of the formation, next to the rugged sandstone cliff that faced the shore. They were sheltered from the eyes of anyone coming down the path to the beach.

As I approached them, I saw Volkov, Zbirak and a small, wiry man I hadn't met. Zbirak was holding a slim laptop computer.

"Mrs. Grace Morrison," Volkov called out to me as I approached. The name grated on my nerves, and I wanted to scream at the SABRE leader that this was not my name. I stopped myself and remembered what Jeremy had said about not getting triggered.

I gripped the folder and the USB stick tightly and held them in front of me.

"It appears you've obeyed my instructions." Volkov

looked up at the cliff, then around the beach in both directions. His face shone with relief. It appeared he was going to get what he'd been expecting for more than two years.

"Good, Mrs. Morrison. You have come alone. I need you to set the stick and the folder down on the rock and back away."

I did as he said. Laid both on the flat rock surface between us, then stepped back.

Zbirak and the thin, wiry man rushed to pick up the stick and folder.

Zbirak opened her laptop then snapped the USB stick into the port on its side. Within a few seconds, her eyes lit up. "It is here!" Then she let loose a stream in a Slavic language and ran to hug Volkov.

The small, wiry man sat on the rock, turning pages one by one in the folder. The lines on his face got deeper as his face pulled into a frown. *"Falshiv dokument!"* he blurted out angrily and threw the folder down on the sand.

Even I could figure out what that meant. I started to feel sick to my stomach.

Volkov ran over and picked up the folder, turning it page by page. He reeled off a stream of words to the small, wiry man in what I figured was Satrovanian. Volkov had an agonized look in his eyes. I at least picked up that the wiry man's name was *Teemo-tee*—or Tim.

Tim shook his head and crossed his arms against his chest. He pointed at me and shook his head. "*Luzhets*!" he said to me, waving his hand at me dismissively, a look of utter scorn on his face.

Volkov turned to me. He pulled the same gun out of his jacket that I'd seen yesterday.

"Timotee has worked on the pipeline maintenance system. He knows it very well, and we brought him for that reason. You and your husband have cheated us, Mrs. Morrison. First you do not give us the codes in Seattle when we came to get them. Now you give us false codes. All of our hopes for our people, gone now!"

Zbirak mumbled something in Satrovanian and came over and spit on the sand in front of me.

Now about ten feet away, Volkov pointed the gun at me. I didn't know whether I should run, duck down, or just prepare to die.

"You are going to shoot me," I said, trying to keep my voice from shaking. "Just like you shot Barb D'Amato in the alley."

A look of puzzlement crossed Volkov's face.

"Mrs. D'Amato?" He frowned and became quiet. He looked over at Zbirak to confirm it. "No, we did not kill her. She was a very friendly lady, and you had just hired her to work at your bakery. She gave us very good information. We gave her money. She brought us a small picture of you and your dog in front of the bakery. We knew it was you, Grace Morrison, working there, just as we suspected."

The only picture of me in front of the bakery was the painting of Biga and me that Beck had made.

I blinked back tears. Maybe it was because my vision had blurred, but I swore I saw a couple with a dog moving into my field of vision. They were edging along the cliffside.

Then in my peripheral vision, I saw a blonde woman with big sunglasses lying down in the sand, commando style, a gun in her hand, aimed at Volkov. I blinked and looked away, not wanting to alert Volkov.

"But you have given us a suggestion, Mrs. Morrison. And today, we are just angry enough to do it."

He held the gun up to me, when I suddenly heard an incredibly loud, deep shout thundering from the cliff above.

It echoed in the cool air. It was not English, but some ancient-sounding Slavic language. I recognized the voice.

"SPREY-tey!"

Volkov turned his head to the cliff top.

"A Satrovanian is here?" His heavy brow furrowed. Puzzled, he looked up again.

At that moment, Volkov was toppled by the commando woman in sunglasses, who looked like a movie star version of a federal agent. She pulled the gun out of his hands easily. A few seconds later, Maura had a gun aimed at Volkov and forced him to lie spread-eagle on the ground, his arms raised.

Zbirak looked at the scene unfolding on the beach and tried to make her escape up the trail to the lot.

As Maura handcuffed Volkov, and Jeremy restrained the still-bewildered Timotee, the blonde woman in the sunglasses ran after Zbirak, who finally let herself be restrained.

The blonde woman took off her sunglasses, and I saw what I should have suspected. It was Renee Westerman, the agents' local operative. The one who'd been keeping an eye on our house for the past week.

She was the one who'd warned the chief last fall that the Russian spies had abducted my dad and me from our house and were taking us to The Laughing Loaf.

If the chief knew about my witness protection status, and what danger I'd been in from SABRE, it was because of her.

I watched Nate nimbly make his way down the sloped part of the cliffside. He jumped down when he was three feet above the sand.

I met him halfway to the cliffside. He ran to me and put his arms around me.

"You speak Satrovanian now?" I smiled wearily and rested my head against his chest. His heart was still pounding. He kissed the top of my head.

"Google Translate actually has Satrovanian. It didn't take much work," he said, with a sheepish smile. "STOP was the only word I looked up."

THE CHIEF MET us in the parking lot above the cove after the three agents brought the handcuffed dissidents up the trail.

I walked over to him. He actually gave me a hug.

"I didn't want to watch this go down. I'm sorry, Gracie. Renee and I disagreed. I didn't think you should have had to go through that."

I sighed and shrugged. "It worked out. And you've probably heard. The Satrovanians didn't kill Barb. I was sure they did."

"I have some information about that. But there's a lot going on right now, and we're about to make an arrest. Can I stop by your house tonight to talk?"

I gulped and nodded. I wanted to know what had happened to poor Barb.

A few minutes later the county sheriff's deputies arrived. We spent a while in interviews with the deputies, explaining how the situation with the codes and Volkov's hunt for me unfolded over the past week. The sheriff interviewed each of the Satrovanians, with the chief standing by. On the word of the agents, Zbirak, Volkov, and Timotee were taken in for more questioning.

"Are they going to be arrested?" I asked the group. "They didn't hurt me."

"Volkov drew a gun on you twice, Gracie," Maura

reminded me. "He looked serious when he said he'd shoot you down there."

"They were caught up in this just like I was." I felt the dissidents had been cheated out of something.

"I think the Satrovanians are going to meet with the State department to discuss other options for dealing with the problems in their country," Jeremy said, taking his beach hat off. "Shutting down the pipeline would not have worked in their favor."

"I hope things change in their country," I said to apparently nobody. The chief was with the sheriff, interviewing the Satrovanians. Jeremy and Maura were laughing as they tried to corral the enthusiastic puppy they'd borrowed.

Nate put his arm around me and held me close. "I hope so, too."

Chapter Twenty-Nine

The chief came over to our house with Renee that night.

I'd brought some chocolate chip cookies home this afternoon from the bakery, which, it turned out, survived very well without me.

Maeve had burned two trays of our precious flatbread, since she'd had to fill in at the front counter. Other than that, the lunch crew of Daisy and Evan handled the crowds well. Beck counted a total of 256 customers throughout the day.

Before the chief and his daughter arrived, I laid the cookies out on a tray and took out small glasses and our bottle of aged port, which I knew the chief enjoyed on occasion--as his one sweet vice.

First, the chief filled me in on what had happened in Boulder Creek in my absence today.

"We knew Barb's payment came from The Satrovanian International Bank," he said. "But we didn't know why—until Volkov confirmed it at the cove. If they were going to kill her anyway, it didn't make sense to me that SABRE, which Renee said struggles on a barebones budget, would have let her cash a big check just to lose that money."

"You're right." I nodded sadly, thinking of how excited Barb must have been to get that money for her business.

"Then Gordon Dabney said the landlord had leased Barb's space without raising the rent. That didn't make sense. Corinne and I went to find out who'd signed the contract. It was Carlene McCaffrey, who was planning to cash in on the success of Mangia Mama by starting her own Italian import food store, *Mangia Mercato*. She cut a deal with the landlords, offering to bring them in as investors.

"Barb found out what her former assistant was planning. When Barb told her she had the money she needed to reopen the shop, Carlene killed her."

"Mangia *Mercato*. Nobody would ever guess she was trying to cash in on Barb's success." I said, rolling my eyes. "So Carlene had a motive. But how do you know she did it?"

The chief leaned forward in his seat. "Amora at the credit union grew up with Carlene. Carlene's dad was a gun collector. He took her out to shoot on weekends. She was a crack shot. Within a few hours, I got a warrant to search her house. She had a 1940s-era Luger from her dad's collection. which looks like it will match the markings on the bullet we found. Brad and I arrested her this afternoon."

Barb's murder was a horrible crime, but it made me feel good that the mayor and chief had figured it out together.

We sat down in the living room and, for about ten minutes, relived today's events at Shark Fin Cove.

"Renee, I would never have guessed you were the fed's local contact." I took a sip of port. "My dad and I have been speculating about the contact's identity for the past year."

"Really." Renee laughed as she picked up another cookie. "I have to know your guesses."

"Well, we thought at first that Reggie McFerrin might be it. Since he's who you'd *least* expect. Like Nate said, a hippie working for the government."

"Oh, that's good," Renee said, stifling a laugh. "I like the way he thinks."

"Then I thought maybe it was Brad Castro."

Renee had just taken a drink of port and almost did a spit take. She set her glass down on the coffee table and began giggling.

"But then Maura and I caught him playing a Pokémon video game on his stakeout behind the bakery."

Renee's face was turning red now, and she was gasping for breath. Even the Chief was laughing.

"I'm glad it was you, Renee." I smiled. "I will never forget the way you went after Volkov when he looked up at Nate on the cliff."

"Nate's timing could not have been more perfect. Seriously, I enjoyed today's showdown. Reminds me how much I love my job." She grinned. "Now if I can just use my agenting skills to figure out who my daughter is dating. She's being quite mysterious with me."

"Oh, I have an idea." This wasn't my news to share. "She'll tell you when she's ready. I think you'll be happy with her choice. She could do worse."

Chapter Thirty

I f you were trying to avoid the crowds, Santa Cruz Beach Boardwalk wasn't the best place to go on a weekend.

After an exhausting two weeks at the bakery, Beck and I had decided to close at noon and drive down on a very hot July Saturday to see Sky Robbins at his summer gig, working the Giant Dipper Coaster.

Since Sam and Nate had no interest in thrill rides, they went on a hike through the redwoods at Henry Cowell State Park instead.

After seeing the long lines for the rides, we decided to buy tickets just for the Giant Dipper. And we knew for sure that Sky was working the ride that day.

The line for the ride wound back and forth in the roped-off maze setup several times. Someone told us that from where we were standing, it would take us an hour to get on the ride.

So we talked. About the bakery, about how the staff was working out. About new baked goods we might want to include on the menu in the future.

Then Beck asked me, nervously, about that Friday when I'd had to leave during lunch time. "You were okay, right? I've never seen you look so scared. I was worried about you."

I kept my voice down. I don't know why; it's not like any of the many teenagers standing around us would care about or know anything about my life.

"I had to take care of some leftover business from my time with ex-husband. It was hard. I dealt with it. It's over and I feel better now."

Beck stared at me, her eyes wide. "You never told me you'd been married, Gracie. Never." She probably didn't know anyone who was divorced—or at least anyone who admitted to being divorced.

"It's probably because I wanted to forget it myself." I saw the look of shock on her face and felt regret. We didn't talk much about personal things at work. "I'm sorry."

"He was not a good person?"

"Not at all." I shook my head. We moved up a few feet in line. "He did some very bad things. He's in prison now."

A look of awe formed on Beck's face as she processed the word *prison*. "I'm so sorry. But now you have somebody better."

"I do." Tears stung my eyes.

"Gracie," she said quietly, running her hand along the rail alongside us as we moved ahead in line. "I didn't get pregnant this month again. I thought it would happen right away. But—well, I just found out last night that it didn't. I cried so hard Sam got scared."

At that, tears started rolling down my face, too. But at this point, I didn't even care. "Oh, Beck."

We hugged until two teenage girls behind us got huffy because we were holding up the line.

"Oh, my *God!*" The two young women flashed us angry looks with their heavily made-up raccoon eyes. "Can you guys just *muh-ooov-ah?*"

Beck and I looked at each other and laughed through our tears.

We finally reached the bright red, curving coaster station and heard Sky droning in a sing-song voice as a train of coaster cars came in.

"Wait till the bar lifts, then exit to your right. Anything you leave in your seats, we will sell for poker money."

"Sky!" We both yelled excitedly.

"Welcome, Laughing Loaf Ladies," he called out and waved us up to the front car of the train. We looked at each other.

"We get the front car!" We squealed together with both fear and excitement.

Sky rolled his eyes and snickered at us.

"Do you think I'd let my friends sit anywhere else?"

We got in and lowered the bar till it locked into place. And then we stared into the black tunnel, the first part of the ride. The great unknown.

We screamed as we surged forward. Then squealed with giddiness as we broke into the bright sunlight. We ratcheted up slowly, coaster wheels clanking below us, to the peak of the ride. As the coaster paused at the top, we looked around during those few seconds of peace to see the beach, the crowds below, and the brilliant blue summer sky.

Then we screamed as we plunged down an amazing dip, with the wooden structure creaking ominously around us.

We leaned into each climb and each fall. Then into each other with every whiplashing turn.

Laughing. Screaming. Then as we pulled into the station, panting with satisfied relief.

As we exited down the stairs, we looked over the crowded rope maze below us.

"We have time to do one more, don't we?" Beck asked, her eyes bright and her cheeks pink.

"It's only an hour wait. Why not?"

And we went to take our place at the end of the line.

THE END

Thank you

Thank you for reading
Shot Through the Tart!

If you enjoyed this book, please consider leaving a review or rating on Amazon, Goodreads or the book review site of your choice.

I truly value the time you take to do this, and it makes my author heart happy.

Also by Victoria Kazarian

Drop Dead Bread - Laughing Loaf Bakery Mystery #1

Bread to Rights - Laughing Loaf Bakery Mystery #2

Trouble You Don't Knead - Laughing Loaf Bakery Mystery #3

Sourdough and Cyanide - Laughing Loaf Bakery Mystery #4

Proof of Death - Laughing Loaf Bakery Mystery #5

An Oven Beyond - Laughing Loaf Bakery Mystery #6

Stop, Drop and Rolls: A Laughing Loaf Bakery Short Mystery
(prequel novella)

TRADITIONAL MYSTERY

writing as VL Kazarian

(Detectives Ruiz, Grasso and Flores):

Swift Horses Racing – Silicon Valley Murder Book 1

Across the Red Sky – Silicon Valley Murder Book 2

A Tree of Poison – Silicon Valley Murder Book 3

About Victoria Kazarian

Victoria Kazarian lives and writes in San Jose, California. After working for years as a Silicon Valley marketing professional, she taught high school English and actually owned a bread bakery of her own called The Laughing Loaf. When she's not writing, she enjoys baking artisan breads and forcing her children and dog to go on road trips to the Pacific Northwest.

See what she's up to at victoriakazarian.com

You can contact Victoria—or perhaps leave a message for Gracie Markley herself—at TheLaughingLoaf@gmail.com

Acknowledgments

Many thanks to my beta readers—Kerry Nozicka, Faye Friesen Myers, and Chris Anderson. Thank you for finding the disappearing dogs and grammar glitches. Special thanks to Chris Anderson, who is the queen of timelines and logic, something that I am not.

Thank you to Karen Stevenson for finding things no one else finds—you have a skill I do not have, and you are a lifesaver.

Thanks to my editor, Honest Magpie, for brainstorming and troubleshooting the plot of this book, as well as watching cheesy movies about small Balkan monarchies on Netflix with me [ahem...*The Christmas Prince*] for inspiration.

To my husband, Pete, thanks as always for your patience and encouragement. And to my children for writing along with me, even though they're writing sci fi, not cozy mystery. They've discovered the secret: writing is fun.

Thanks to you, my readers, for following the adventures of Gracie and The Laughing Loaf Bakery through these books. I love hearing what you've liked and what characters are your favorites. I plan to keep this series going for while, so if you run into a cliffhanger at the end of a book, just know there will be another book in which it will be resolved!

As always, thanks to the Sisters in Crime Coastal

Cruisers chapter—the write-ins, encouragement, and companionship are invaluable in a profession where we are spinning stories in a cave by ourselves. Let's keep doing it!

Are you in a book club?

Interested in reading any of The Laughing Loaf Bakery Mysteries with your book club? I'd love to appear at your book club online - and possibly in person, if you're in the San Francisco Bay Area.

Contact me at thelaughingloaf@gmail.com

Laughing Loaf Bakery Recipes

Strawberry Shortcake Tarts
How to Score Bread Loaves

Beck's Strawberry Shortbread Tarts (with Creme Anglaise)

Total time: About 2-3 hours

You can make these in steps, since the crust dough can chill in the fridge for a couple of days until you bake it. The creme anglaise can also chill in a sealed container in the fridge for a couple of days.

Crust

1 ¼ cup all-purpose flour
⅓ cup powdered sugar
¼ teaspoon salt
½ cup (1 stick) chilled butter, cut into pieces
1 egg yolk
1 tablespoon heavy cream
½ teaspoon vanilla bean paste

Combine flour, powdered sugar, and salt in a food processor. If you don't have a food processor, you can also use a pastry blender or two forks. Add the cut up butter and pulse or blend until it looks crumbly. Combine the egg yolk, heavy cream, and vanilla bean paste in a dish, then process or blend it into the main mixture until the dough rolls into a ball. If you need to, add a few drops of cream to make it come together.

Press the dough into a roll, like refrigerated cookie dough. Wrap in plastic and chill in the fridge for 30 minutes

Before you're ready to bake, spray tins with baking spray or grease them with a paper towel soaked lightly with oil or butter.

If you're using 3-1/2" tart tins, cut your roll of dough into 6 pieces. If you're using cupcake tins, you can cut it into about 10 pieces. Sprinkle each cut piece lightly with flour and then roll till about 1/4-1//2" thin with a rolling pin. Press into a mold with your fingers, but be careful to keep the thickness consistent. Use a fork to poke the crust a few times in the middle so it won't rise up during baking.

Freeze the tart shells for about 30 minutes, then bake them in a 350°F (190°C) oven for about 15 minutes or until they're light golden brown.

Creme Anglaise

1 cup cream
1 1/2 cups whole milk
1/2 cup granulated sugar, divided evenly into two bowls
1 tablespoon vanilla bean paste
6 egg yolks

In a medium, heavy-bottomed saucepan add the cream, whole milk, 1/4 cup sugar, <u>and vanilla bean paste.</u>

Simmer over medium heat until the mixture starts to bubble just at the edges, for about 2 minutes, but do not let it boil. Remove from the heat and let it stand for 20 minutes.

In a medium bowl, whisk the egg yolks with the remaining 1/4 cup of sugar.

You'll now temper the eggs, so they won't curdle. To do this, ladle some of the warm cream mixture into the egg yolk mixture, then whisk to combine. Add another ladle of the cream mixture to the eggs until the egg mixture is warm to the touch.

Pour the tempered cream-and-egg mixture into the remaining cream in the saucepan, then return the pan to the heat.

Now cook this mixture over medium heat, stirring constantly until the custard coats the back of a spoon. This will take about 5 to 7 minutes. The mixture will thicken.

Now remove from the heat and strain through a fine sieve into a medium bowl to remove any lumps. Place the custard pan in a bath of ice cubes and water to stop it from cooking any further. Chill the creme anglaise in the fridge until it's cool enough to fill your tart.

Strawberries

Wash and cut up your strawberries, then mix in a table-spoon and a half of honey and about two teaspoons of lemon zest. Mix thoroughly and chill.

To assemble

Spoon chilled creme anglaise into each baked and cooled tart shell, spreading it out till it's about 1/2 inch thick. Then top with strawberries and whipped cream (or whipped topping of your choice). We sprinkle cut pieces of mint over the top of the whipped cream.

How to Score Bread

Scoring bread creates a nice design on your loaf as it bakes. It can be simple or it can be very detailed. My advice is to start simple. This is a learning experience, and you will get better the more you do it.

Get a lame

The best thing to use is what Gracie uses in The Laughing Loaf: a *lame* (pronounced lahm). They're inexpensive and easily found on Amazon or any baking website. A lame holds a razor blade and allows you to maneuver the blade quickly and without hurting yourself.

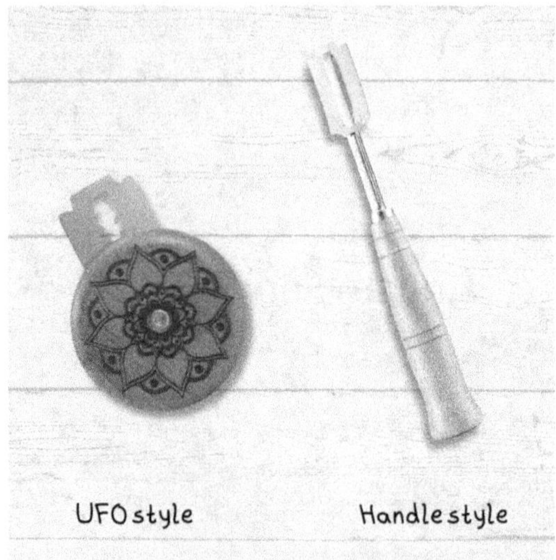

There are two styles available:

• On the left: the round "UFO" style, which grasps the razor blade in a circular holder.
• On the right: the handle style—which fits a razor blade into its end.

It's a personal preference, but most bakers I know find they can make quicker, easier cuts with the UFO style.

Here are some things to remember when scoring your loaf:
There are two reasons to score a loaf

- To allow it to expand during baking
- To make an artistic design.

If you want to do an artistic design, it's best to do that,

then include an "ear" cut or "box" cut that will allow your loaf to expand during baking without causing your pretty design to get bloated by expanding too much during baking.

1. Scoring is the last thing you'll do before baking!

Your loaf should be fully proofed. Make sure your oven is at baking temperature before you score.

2. Score when the loaf is COLD

If you've been making a cold-rise sourdough loaf (as in the recipe in the back of *Sourdough and Cyanide*) your loaf should already be cold.

But if you're making a biga or other loaf with a warm proof, you'll need to firm up your loaf before scoring. While your oven is preheating, pop the loaf in the freezer for about 15 minutes until the surface has firmed up.

3. Lightly dust the top of the cold loaf with flour, then smooth it over lightly with your hand.

4. Dip the lame blade in water first and make quick cuts in the loaf of about 1/4"-1/2" inch deep.

5. Do not drag the blade as you're cutting. Cut it quickly. You should be pulling it through the dough smoothly, not tearing it in any way.

6. Get your bread into the oven as soon as you've finished scoring, since it quickly starts to expand as soon as it's cut!

Some simple scoring designs

Simple Parallel Lines

(The two loaves on the upper left corner of the square)
My favorite, easy design is simply to cut 4-5 parallel lines of
1/4-1/2" inch deep, about 3/4" inch apart down the loaf.
This works as an expansion cut but also looks nicely
decorative.

The Cross

(Upper right hand corner)
Cut one line down the middle of the loaf, then cut another
perpendicular line across it. This is an expansion cut. It lets

the loaf expand but also ends up looking very professional after baking.

The Box

(The right-most loaf in the lower right photo)
Cut four lines in the center of the loaf, creating a square that takes up most of the flat surface of the loaf. This is an expansion cut, since the square will raise up during baking as the loaf expands. It also gives you some space inside the box to do a small leaf design—cut a straight line, then on either side of the line, cut 3-4 short lines at a 45 degree angle.

The Ear

(Lower left loaf)
This is an expansion cut and will open up your loaf in a big way as it bakes. You can just use this cut—or you can do a small or narrow design on the opposite side of the loaf from the ear cut. To do the ear cut, start with the lame at the upper side of the loaf, just an inch or two in, holding the lame at a 30 degree angle. Pull it down at 1/2-3/4 inch deep, the whole length of the loaf.

The Leaf

(below)

Another fairly easy design is the leaf. First cut a line down the middle of the loaf at 1/4" inch deep. Then on either side of this center line, cut four or five deeper lines at a 45 degree angle to the center line. Then cut a 1/2" deep line around this figure, in the shape of a leaf. This leaf cut will give room for the loaf to expand. As a finishing touch, you can make quick little cuts around the circumference of the loaf.

Here are some YouTube channels to check out for scoring inspiration:

<u>Foodgeek</u> - Sourdough scoring techniques

<u>Bread Journey</u> - more detailed scoring techniques (they're beautiful but a little advanced)

Shot Through the Tart Playlist

To enjoy singing along with the tunes Gracie, Beck, Maeve, and Rose sing as they bake, listen to the *Shot Through the Tart* playlist on Spotify. Includes fun songs from the late 1980s and early 1990s suggested by Laughing Loaf Mystery fans.

Shot Through the Tart playlist

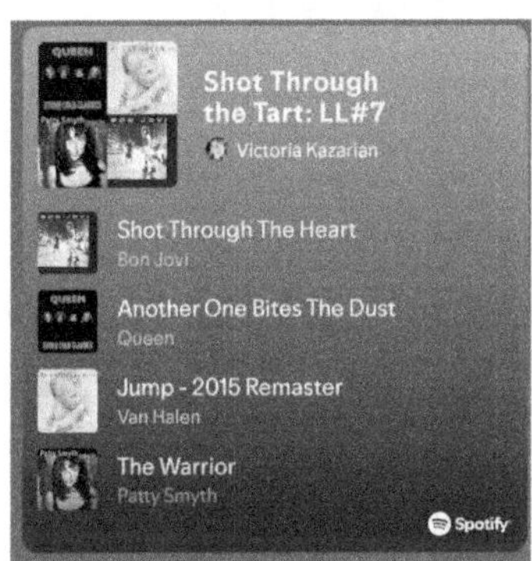